MOLOTOV MOUTHS
Explosive New Writing

MOLOTOV MOUTHS
Explosive New Writing

James Tracy, Dani Montgomery,
Raw Knowledge, George Tirado,
Leroy Moore, Ananda Esteva, and
Josiah Luis Alderete

Manic D Press
San Francisco

The Molotov Mouths Outspoken Word Troupe performs live at schools, festivals, libraries, readings, and cultural events throughout the US and Canada. To purchase their spoken word CD *Poetically Correct, Politically Direct* or for booking information, contact molotovmouths@riseup.net.

Illustration: Eric Drooker
Cover design: Yolanda Montijo

Library of Congress Cataloging-in-Publication Data

Molotov mouths : explosive new writing / James Tracy ... [et. al].
    p. cm.
ISBN 0-916397-87-4 (alk. paper)
1. Protest literature, American—California—San Francisco.
2.American literature—California—San Francisco. 3. Politics, Practical—Literary collections. 4. Social problems—Literary collections. 5. American literature—21st century. I. Tracy, James.
  PS572.S33M65 2003
    810.8'0358'0976491—dc21

2003014573

CONTENTS

new writing by

If there were ever a time for Molotov Mouths, it's now. Speak books, speak pens, speak songs, speak and never stop speaking until we get the balance, abundance, and justice this much-battered world deserves. Dissent and more dissent — until the planet melts or we find our way to a realized state of harmony and cooperation. Our choice.

— Luis J. Rodriguez

ANANDA ESTEVA was born in Chile and raised in the San Francisco Bay Area. A gifted storyteller, she intertwines bilingual poetry and song to paint a picture of life in Las Americas. She has performed and published internationally, and co-authored *Poetry for the People*.

SCENT OF MAGNOLIA

> *There's a humming in the air*
> *Billie Holiday's "Strange Fruit"*
> *haunting like a mischievous wind*
> *and then I begin my poem.*

How can we rise up
when we're locked up?
How can we rise up
when we're locked up?
Look around
There are holes in our communities
holes where our folks once stood in plain view.
Now it's all about visiting hours
and letters
with prison identification numbers
on the lines
where the names should go.

The 13th Amendment
wrapped around our necks
"... neither slavery nor involuntary servitude
except
as punishment for a crime."

The news and movies show us the violent crimes
desperate brown faces
with bloodshot eyes
folks that bring fear to some and shame to others
folks we don't want to see.
We got over two million people incarcerated in the US in 2003

Mostly for crimes of poverty
Like single mamas making $5,000 a year
busted for check fraud
at the grocery store.
And crimes of coincidence
like how Sheila was in the car with José who had mota in his
mochilla
next thing you know
they're both doing time.

Two million holes in our communities,
that's like the city of San Francisco
gone underground
working on the chaingang
in Arizona & Louisiana
building silicon chips in Califas
workin' in the fields in Oregon
two million captive workers
two million holes.

It's weird riding the bus
hearing about this brother locked up
that brother on trial
this granddaddy over here
esta hija
that son
esa mama.
And folks talk about it like it's an everyday thing.
The conversation rolls on
talking about shopping the next breath
talking about what are you doing next weekend?

And I think about the collect calls from the block
And how many times my parents hung up.
"No, we do not accept these charges!
You'll never learn if we do."
And how most of the time
I tried to forget about my cousins in prison.
I never told anybody.
It's like they never existed.

How can we rise up when we're locked up?
The 13th Amendment got us strung up
tied tight around our necks
cutting out breath
shutting out voice
no civil rights to shout about
just the
    bulging eyes and the twisted mouth
Ms. Holiday sung about back in the '50s

Her song whistles and screams
through the holes in our communities.
Her song rattles street signs in Philly
blows up leaves in Birmingham
creates cracks along the sidewalk in Queens.
    strange fruit hanging from the poplar trees
the sound echoes
through those holes in our communities
where our folks once stood.
You know this song well.
It's the buzzing in your walls
the humming in Taos
that chill between your shoulder blades.
Can you hear it?
TVs, cell phones, refrigerators drown it out.
    Scent of magnolia sweet and fresh
Did you hear it?

How can we rise
how can we rise...
How can we rise up when we're plugged up... and plugged in?
TVs   Cell Phones
competing sounds drown out the calls of our folks on the inside
The news tells us it's our fault and
Let the rotten apples rot in jail
We breathe in those lies
'til we believe 'em
But Billie's song cries on
urging us to remember

the connections
that old rope tying us to the past
stretching back to the time when the lynching started
right after the 13th Amendment
the end of slavery and the beginning
of the prison industrial complex

> *These are the fruit for the crows to pluck*
> *For the rain to gather*
> *For the wind to suck*
> *For the sun to rot*
> *For the trees to drop*
> *These are a strange and bitter crop.*

ROLLING HILLS MEMORIAL PARK

I.

In the North Richmond flatlands you gotta watch your back, do the gooseneck strut: two looks forward 'n one look back. In the Rich-Town flatlands you come as easy as money; easy to come by, easy to burn. Too many brothers shot down in Rich-Town. Their bones lay to rest in Rolling Hills Memorial Park. Our African-American Studies teacher used to warn us to watch out and stick to the books not to the sidewalks or we might end up another colored body at the Rolling Hills Cemetery, too many brothers' bones lay to rest there already.

My teacher wasn't talking directly to me: female, light skinned, sometime passing for White, but to me as a member of a larger community. I lived right by those Rolling Hills and I witnessed procession after procession; limousines lined up rolling in slow through those wrought metal gates where all the mourners pass through. I watched folks dressed in fine linen suits and Sunday best, white collars, white stockings, and an occasional fan as they came to pay respects.

II.
One day coming home from school
the bus sticks to the road
in a sudden stop

nowhere to roll
when double-dutch rows of dark cars with dark windows
and long limousines
cover the two lane road
starting at the cemetery entrance all the way down to the
freeway
everybody stuck
forced to take a moment and breathe
look around to see amber coals staining everything with
evening glow

One man steps out of a limo and stands up
in the middle of the road
his back to the cemetery
he faces the sun's slow march down over the western hills
I watch him through the bus window
he's tall and regal in a golden silk suit
that reflects the colors of the sky
so he becomes the sun on earth

This man stand right there in the middle of the road
his body blocks the on-coming cars
their honking makes a crazy waving music
but the man stand still
his ears don't hear the horns
he hear another voice singing
I can tell by the way he sway his head
and shuts his eyes

Some cars try to pass him
but he stand there solid
he won't move
baby nephew getting restless
twisting and whining in his car seat
but he stand there
a rock in the river
a rock with roots to the center of the earth
he stand there
in the middle of the road
watching the sun go down

he stand there
listening
a chief looking over his people
cherishing their step and sway
remembering days of feast and dance
remembering stories his great-great-grandmother passed down
of how his people came to be
these stories sound like songs
like poetry

And he stand there
his wife gets out of the car
she take his hand
and stand alongside of him
blocking traffic together
watching the sun burn over Mount Tam
cuz if they don't take this moment
who will remember their son
the Black man's body count up one
toward the fifty percent to be dead or in jail by the year 2010

From my seat in the bus I watch them
through scratched up plexi-glass I watch them
I can hear a music I cannot name
but I feel the beats sound in my chest
The Voice fills my lungs with an ancient air
and I know this old time music been feeding my spirit all these
    years
I just forgot to listen until now

This music makes the world stop
car horns get quiet
angry voices tumble into silence
we all don't move
we all painted gold
while the sky cries in crimson colors
wailing, wailing this old song
a song that heals all those who find a way to listen
the wind stop her whining and rustling
to hear The Song

and even Time take a moment
to watch this young man's spirit pass
over the western hills
n join the sky

If this man didn't stand up for his son and stop the world
who knows if the usual graveside prayer
could fill his empty chest
he had to stand there
and watch his son's spirit rise up into the sky
remember his roots
sing that old song
he stand there solid
a rock in the river
a rock with roots to the center of the earth
he stand there
in the middle of the road
watching the sun go down
watching his baby fly on to the other side
he stand there
till the sky shed her red color
and turn into the dark of night
he stand there in protest
cuz if he don't honor his son
who will?
he stand there
he stand there
he stand

MEMORIAS CHILENAS/ CHILEAN MEMORIES

I was two years old
when death threats
forced us to flee Chile
travel north to Gringo-landia-USA
where you expect me to forget
my culture and assimilate
along with all the other lost souls here

stripped of their history
"at such a young age
you can't possibly know your country.
You're American now" you say

No I cannot spout out
the names of Chileno heroes
or the rivers
or even the tallest peak in the Andes
I sure can't dance La Cueca
or La Marinera
though their rhythms run through my bones and feed me

And yes I got to escape 17 years of dictatorship
a half-sleep nightmare
thick in the air like fog
I got to escape

You look at me
and see no traces of the past
I speak perfect English
most of the time
and sport a smile
you can't see the memories
I drag along with me
what they do to my thoughts
you don't hear my voice
coated and quaky with fear
don't notice the dull
film over my eyes
as they travel back in time
back in time
to the year 1973

The blood I saw as a baby
seeps into my memory
and flows into my mind
this blood stains my eyes
I see everything thru
red lenses

red birds rush across a
blood streaked sky
who's after them
I wonder
will they make it?

I see red in your face
red drops oozing out your nose
dripping down your cheek
but I go on talking
don't skip a beat
I don't wanna seem like I'm crazy now

I see bodies
pale and bloated
floating down the Mapocho River
bodies of socialists, of teachers, doctors,
poor folk, your folk, and poets
immersed in swirling waters
red foam residue

I see the body of Mamá's friend Emanuel
he refused to doctor Pinochet's Army
"I took an oath to serve the people... the people" he chanted
then the soldiers smashed his hands with a hammer
bones splinter
"Now let's see you perform surgeries on YOUR people!"
they laughed and let him go
three weeks later
someone found him face down in the river
the Mapocho River

His body floats into my dreams
his red lips move
but I hear no sound
"¡Emanuel! ¡Emanuel!
¡Háblame Emanuel!"

I see red when the police pull us over
red bruises on my face

just appear on their own
red wounds on my breasts
where the men cut me with little knives
just for fun
where they inserted red hot wires
to make me talk

Every time I see a cop
I hang my head low
so not to see my reflection in his Ray-Bans
my red reflection
as seen through my blood-stained eyes
this stain I can't seem to shake
despite all these years
living in this Gringo culture of forgetting

So when you tell me
I was too young to remember Chile
I want you to look into my eyes
look   look deep
look until you feel yourself traveling back in time
to the year 1973
look until you see yourself as a baby, as me
looking up at my Mama's vacant gray eyes
watching her put a wet cloth over my mouth
to protect me from tear gas
take note now
which corner do we go
to hide from their bullets?
if you look deep enough
you will know too
if you dare to look
maybe they'll start shooting at you
if you stare into my eyes
you should hear the sound of women wailing
calling out the names of their children
Los Desaparecidos
listen
to the rumble of their running feet
to the sound

of other feet pursuing
with a steady synchronized rhythm
mechanized hunters
charging through my memories
tracking us down
me and my loved ones
my community
how can I forget?
this blood I saw as a baby
has grown with me
sewn into my skin
permanent sutures
how can I forget?
the red memories follow me
up and down the street
don't tell me I don't remember my country
I live it
every
day

DOESN'T MATTER WHAT YOU'VE LIVED THROUGH I MAKE YOU VERDE IN MY ARMS

verde
que te quiero **verde**
green I want you green
when I say **verde**
I'm not just talking about the color
and Lorca
the guy who cried these words the first time
he had other things on his mind

verde que te quiero **verde**
verde carne
verde pelo

I want your body
green as the last jungle canopy

I want your skin green
your hair
I want your touch
green like a meadow in the springtime
now do you know what I mean?
green isn't just a color
it's a way of saying
I'm fresh and plump on the vine
and I'm firm
noonday sun hasn't beaten me down to a pulp
cuz I won't let him

some people say **verde** for unripe fruit
but baby it's our word now
and I'm telling I'm **verde** not
cuz I been hiding behind a leaf
my whole life
when I was 16 I thought I'd seen it all
I let boys do whatever they wanted
with my body
I let girls say whatever they wanted
about my body
I wasn't **verde**
n I carried them with me
I carried them with me
in my tired swollen body
pero te digo que estoy **verde**
verde viviente

green like hot summer rain
tearing through your clothes
running down your body
hot summer rain is **verde**
and you know I'm feeling **verde**

just ease into the **verde** breeze
doesn't matter what you've lived through
I make you **verde** in my arms
verde carne
verde piel

YO GHETTO LUV

Yo ghetto luv
cut roads in my body
harsh white roads like desert
creeping into my jungle
before I know it
you in
slashing and burning my best trees
yo huge ruff hands snag 'cross my skin
sound like bulldozers
you trample through my lands like
Señor Conquistador
uprooting medicine plants
you need to save yo life

M'ijo
yo ghetto love cut
roads in my body
cuz yo ghetto life cut roads in yo soul
n the fuckers from the group home
still tryin' to wedge their way 'tween yo legs
you trying to fight them
thru my body
gotta fight
you pin me down in the corna
bam slam
in the corna
left hand
sunk in my thigh
yo right at my neck
n you don't see
how deep you diggin' into me
you don't see my curves
don't feel my nerves
jumping and screamin' and STOP

but your eyes gone grazin' in past pastures
chewing on garbage dump grasses
over there where they built the projects

where we used to live
where I learned to hate ghetto luv
but believe I don't deserve no betta

Baby, yo ghetto luv
cut roads in my body
look at me
I dare you to look at me
I'm more than just a plot of land
you think you own
I'm more than just a woman
my jungle spread
all across the earth
my toes dipped in ocean
my hair touch the sky
my tears rain down
thru your broken roof
don't you see?
you're tramplin'
on hallowed ground here
la tierra sagrada que es mi cuerpo
my body is a sacred land

I been kicked around so much so young
it took me this long to learn
I don't need to take this from you
it's a part of my healing to have my own back
part of my healing to fight for my body
lanzas, escudos, flechas
on my knees through the night
that's right   I'm down for myself too
not just defending my sister   but me
I am my sister and my sister's keeper
defiendo mi tierra
de noche de día de noche de día
yo defiendo mi tierra
porque es mía porque es mía

la defiendo de noche
la defiendo de día
de día me ayuda el viento

de noche las tres Marías
ay ay ay ay ay
so step back
I'ma take back
la tierra sagrada que es mi cuerpo
step back   step back now
or I'ma bust up concrete
turn over yo bulldozers
I'ma bury your roads in my deep earth
let loose a colony of blue poison frogs
n if you don't stop
I'ma drown you in my rivers: El Amazona, El Putumayo,
El Pinche Tu Madre
because my land
is no place
to disrespect

THE PAYBACK FOR 509 YEARS

Yo soy tu Mamá,
tu abuelita
tu hermana
yo soy tu commadre en la lucha
vengo del río
de la tierra
del viento
y tú vienes de mi vientre[1]
I gave birth to you
n now you pretend to be my Papa
so you can tell me what to do
my spirit stretches back 509 years
before the first Conquistador
tore up this sacred ground

----

1   I am your mother, your grandmother, your sister, and I am
your comrade in the struggle. I come from the river, from the
earth, from the wind, and you come from my womb.

I got my hands in the earth
my head in the sky
high enough to see what's really going on
you know like a falcón
I got perspective
I been watching you for 509 years
but you don't stop n ask what I see
nobody do
I'm so used to nobody asking
I don't speak no more
I'm not supposed to talk
until spoken to right
that's what the Man's been sayin'
for 509 years
'cept for tonight
tonight I talk
Sí Señor
I tell you how you caught me
with a big iron hook
can't you see it piercing my cheek?
look carefully
see my blood dripping slow
there it is
I'm out of my element
in your filthy cities
struggling for air
I'm chokin' on your lies
lies that tell me
my female intelligence
don't stand up to yours
my indigenous intelligence
bent over in submission
sure don't stand up to yours
how can I stand up straight
after you cut off my great-great-grandma's feet?
the wounds cross through generations
wounds from the Conquista
509 years ago
don't pretend
you didn't do those things

Remember? I been watching you for 509 years
a falcón in the branches
of the tallest tree
listen to me
you need to know how your lies tied up my body
in old ropes dipped in Catholic guilt
guilt that makes me hate my body
too round for your magazines
but not too thick for your dick
I hear your whispers in my ear
lies telling me you own my body
that's right! like you own your horse
I got a bit in my mouth now
a bit with spikes
biting into my gums
every pinch of pain remind me that you own me again
and you ride me
you ride me hard
into the desert
no water
you just ride me into the earth
then you call me a dirty whore
n you capture another woman
and ride her off over the mountain
you tell her she's your baby doll
the only one you ever wanted
and I
laid out on the ground
my wounds spilling
dry blood mixed with dirt
but you forget
my spirit stretches back 509 years
I got my hands in the earth
we heal each other
and the earth,
she's my abuelita
la tierra
n I take revenge for the way
you tore her up
and the wind

he's my breath
you better watch out
tornado warning tonight
winds spinning round you
lift you up into the sky
cuz I'm bout to fight
fight back with my voice
my breath
my words will pick you off
you and your brothers
one by one
I'm taking aim
you better run
I'm pointing with my finger too
my arm stretched out
pointing at you
like the Boricua slaves
pointing at their masters
a gesture disguised in dance
designed to dole out retribution
the payback for 509 years
of slavery
509 years
of invasion
of violación
509 years
I been waiting
waiting to talk
the wind back me up
the earth
hold me up
my voice been hiding out
for 509 years
building up pressure
but tonight
I talk
tonight
I tell you how it is
how it been for 509 years

WIDE SHOULDERS

I got wide shoulders
a woman's round mountain hips
bulging butt
and sidesweeping strut

you better make way!

I got a man's muscle back
belting biceps
and wide wide shoulders
that don't match
the rest of me
according to Elle, Vogue, Latina and even Ebony
in case you haven't noticed
young Latinas and Black women
coming in smaller and smaller sizes each year
to fit into MTV hootchie,
New York/Frisco Hipster look
or Anne Taylor Yuppie
veering away
from soul food and pozole
their Gramma's would make
time for Slim Fast, Jenny Craig
or the poor-girl version
the "No Food Fast" Diet

it's in style to waste away
teetering on tacones and platform shoes to barely walk
let alone run
skinny tube arms
that can't fight back
forget that!
I got my Gramma's strong arms
broad shoulders
to bear the world on my back if I have to
and the way things are going
I may have to

we throw our health away
just to look a certain way   we don't
we been bought and sold
and sold self-hate
that hatred brews in our bodies like acid
chewing on bone
sucking up blood
biting chunks of heart
leaving us tired
leaving us empty
leaving us with nothing but to look outside ourselves for love
down aisles of clothes and accessories meant to fit someone else
and there we go again
trying to zip up those pants
wishing we been born with long
itty bitty bones
hating our mothers for their curves
hating Abuela's ancestral food
hating the smell of greens n smoked turkey, grits n butterfat
but honey, if you don't eat breakfast
what you gonna do?

You gotta look back in time
to survive the times
look back in time
to survive
these times when we have less than
we ever did
look back
Yemayá te está llamando
en tus sueños
diciéndote que tú
tienes que quererte
a tí misma
no trates de ser
lo que no eres
Look back
look back to your Zapoteca grandmother
and grandmother's grandmother
bién formaditas con curvitas y qué

thick arms carrying baskets
ceramic jugs
balanced on their heads just so
never conquered by the Aztecas or the Spanish
an Indigena nation of
wide women honored for their strength for their savvy
spirit food keep them going
elote, atole, huitlacoche, pozole
These same women
driving the picket lines
las marchas los gritos
As the Zapotecas continue to fight
this next wave of colonization
from the WTO and World Bank
stickin' their noses up into the Ithsmus
wanting to take trees and oil
and sell them images of
    emaciated Anglo women
in return for natural resources
in return for culture
for a sense of history
for homeland
raizes
peregrino
tierra sagrada

We pa' el Norte, already bought up those images
long time ago
gobbled them down
our last meal
we been bought and sold
and sold self-hate
that hatred brews in our bodies like acid
no telling what the damage be
girls running around too hungry to tell
what they paid for 'em
those images that don't match
our mirrors
girls looking outside themselves for love
looking down aisles of clothes

meant to fit someone else
tripping on high heels
too tired to stand up again
to fight the next blow
and it's coming
the attack
well on its way
the fist already balled up
aiming for our faces
calling out our names
it's coming
are you ready to fight?

JOSIAH LUIS ALDERETE is a full-blooded Pocho Indian who refries his beans and poemas in Spanglish. Although a proud son of San Francisco's Mission District, he currently resides in a giant pinata somewhere in East Oakland.

VALENCIA STREET MEMORIES

Walk down Valencia Street, walk down Valencia Street, yeah, I used to walk down Valencia Street... Counting the whiskers on each chin that were dyed red or green or blue or goth-type black and thumbtacked to the pierced lips and tribal methamphetamine tattoo types who used to sit with them other barstool types over there at the Chameleon on a Friday, on a Tuesday, on a Thursday again.

Looking in the windows that got the morning reflected in them and checking out the boarded up ones, the busted up ones, too. Checking out the brujos and pachucos sitting in the open ones, leaning on them tiny fire escapes like plastic santos pointing and whistling and laughing at all the tinfoil burritos, black cups of coffee, torn up used up books that ended up around here, and back then I could meet you after work for a smoke and a beer.

But these days under el quinto sol like a fashionable prophecy predicting the coming of something, them barstools are almost all gone, taken up by some record spinning Beastie Boy clone with his wallet chain attached to his khaki hipbone (and just like the fashionable prophecy said "there's a whole lot of them...."). They brought along their dates for the evening, for the lifetime, for the trend imported from the Marina and brought here to Valencia Street. Coming out of the cabs two by two like animals from the ark, packing urban decay, makeup packets in the pockets of their latest '70s leather jackets. At least a couple times a day they walk right past, and we walk right past, right there on Valencia Street.

That guy selling pieces of himself laid out on a towel by the coffee shop, or maybe you walked right by that one Marvin Gaye -singing crackhead or the Redman or that other crazy brother. Those dudes have been here way before it all; and they'll be here on Valencia Street after the fall of the whole dotcom thing.

Still counting it as it goes from one finger to something for sale over to the next day to the second finger back to the other hand and over to a superstition that used to say, "No way do you want to pass time in that kind of neighborhood," and then that went and passed into a neighborhood that's getting too expensive to pass the time in.

It's that great American pastime we're in: Y'know, can you guess how many gumballs are in that jar? Can you guess how many cholos just drove by in that car on Valencia Street?

Well, how the fuck should I know how many cholos just drove by in that car? I do know that on the day I moved in upstairs behind the stairs of that pan dulce shop, on that day I came so close, so fucking close to having that exact number on the tip of my tongue. But just like that or maybe it was just like this, too many things got confused in the move. I got sidetracked, distracted by the cultures, the shit going on around here.

The slang being snuck past in the palmas of so many hands on Valencia Street going right under the bare bone bar sign bones of the Irish who vacated a while back, while chiva balloons float in the mouths around here, while beers get drunk around here, while the ninos walking with their parents hold back some of what they got to dream and scream about around here.

Y esos son las partes de Valencia Street that keeps the concrete meek and the people real. These everyday parts that bleed and heal are the parts of Valencia Street that are still here over there drying at the laundromat. Over at Sam's liquor store wondering where I'm at. Misplaced along with them old poetry notebooks of mine that I used to wrap up in duct tape like pipe bombs that would explode years later. While them guys in red and black jackets sprouted up on Valencia Street next to them valet parking signs which was the beginnings of the latest trend (the fashionable prophecy) associated with this street so divine.

The too good-looking for TV patrons get into their cars and get asked "Sir, was everything fine? Was the food good? Was the food good?"

Hey, I hear the food is really good around here on Valencia Street. While I slept past noon and stopped with the bent spoon and had my entire Sundays in Dolores Park to think. Years before I'd be washing my dead friend's coffee grounds off the kitchen sink and for me those are the parts of Valencia Street that they're never going to put in that brochure written by that young entrepreneur telling you where you should shop on Valencia Street. Telling you where you shouldn't stop on Valencia Street. While I bought an old-looking new shirt from the guy on the corner, checked out the hooker in the plastic leather skirt, scored a rock from up the block and then smoked it right up, right behind that SUV that's filled with dotcomers in retro clothing that are part of a growth industry on Valencia Street.

I got to tell you, seeing that was the ugliest most prophetic thing I'd seen in a while - I had to go home after seeing that. First I stopped off over at Sam's and bought some of them religious candles that he's got over there by the laundry detergent. And I put them by my alarm clock in an unusually superstitious turn and I let those candles burn and burn and burn...

For the native around here, for the ghost of the Irish around here, for the graffiti artist with a tattoo tear around here, for the working class madre who's got the fear around here.

It's of not being able to pay what's due cuz that couple dressed in J Crew are looking nicer brighter whiter than you and are looking for a cute new space.

I let those candelas burn and burn and burn for the few gutter punks y street poets still left in this place (Bucky Sinister, Swanny, The Pigeonman, George Tirado - presente).

Still walking down Valencia Street still heaven sent and go ask the ghost of Jack Micheline where he went on Valencia Street - and I got to tell you that after all this time... Something inside of me is still here; something inside mi corazon went "click"; something tangible that you could shake a stick at.

What I'm trying to say is that I felt something after all that, I felt something for this street. I felt something for Valencia Street. Walking home all alone I kicked at the #26 bus cuz I'd gotten baptized, I'd gotten converted by some kind of sermon... Whose words are the sidewalk cracks; whose words hold up the telephone poles and hold open the café doors; whose words make up the trendy new bars and them smooth new cars parked in the middle of Valencia Street. On a Friday, on a Tuesday, on a Thursday again....

SHOPPING FOR LA CULTURA

Well, I love it over there at the Mexican market and la senora behind the counter's got a gold virgen santa locket and I always end up over there on Thursday buying mangos y media libra de queso fresco. Whenever I walk by the Cafe Bustelo I always stop and eyeball them cereal boxes of chocopuffs.

Cuz I swear that that monkey on the box used to be a heroin dealer in my old neighborhood and if I been lucky and if I been good all week there will be fresh homemade corn tortillas like the kind my abuelita didn't use to make.

Over there wrapped in plastic next to the chiclets y packets of funky dried fishcakes y no disrespect meant here y'hear but y'know that senora I was telling you about with the gold virgen santa locket? Well, every time I come in here she's wearing some eres chacone outfit with her breasts about ready to pop out of their sockets. Sometimes held back behind the counter by nothing more than a black push-up bra and since she's about my ma's age it makes me blush when I see what I just saw. She's got the kind of jewelry on I always imagine Jackie Collins would have if Jackie Collins shopped at La Pulga, if Jackie Collins shopped at La Segunda. Her long nails click-clack against the register keys and she smiles at me, asks me if I got everything for the week and there's some chicarones in this metal bowl today, all wet and greasy sitting next to the register on the counter.

"Y estan acabados de hacer," she says to me and when I look up I start to get dizzy cuz I notice Pokeman piñatas and stuff like that, bright ceramic galios and Jesus Christo piggybanks that I swear I seen in my dreams poking at Godzilla's eyes like it was some Japanese monster movie scene.

Carnival cartoon angelitos been circling our heads this whole time on that top shelf overhearing our prayers and grocery lists. Maybe smooshing them all together into one big continuous "Que vayas con dios" while you're there don't forget the Uncle Ben's arroz.

Y que la virgen te bendiga tu queso cotija y cajeta tan rica
y padre nuestro que estas en el cielo...

Wasn't it you who told me that Juan Diego endorses this brand of tamales?

Y ponte trucha or no valle mano
y que te llege mucho jalle mano.

So you can pay for all this stuff that seems to be accumulating in your shopping cart, in your pockets, in the trunk of your car, in your hermana's closet, in the cracks of the culture.

Unless of course you got nine items or less, in which case the express lane will bless your abuelito's Tecate limon and bag of Fritos y que suenes con los angelitos down here where everything is being surrounded by these big ass Mexican chicks in these posters advertising beer, these girls in red in Tecate cutouts smiling all big, saying, "This is what it's all about, papi..."

I'm looking at this and I'm looking at that and I look up and down the little aisles at all this sanctified cultural consumerism. I see myself reflecting back in the Corona mirror, the Carta Blanca mirror, the Bohemia mirror. I get all caught up in the moment and think to myself, "Man, this is all holy as hell." I get down on my knees and I buy some of those chicarones even though they don't go down too well, even though I don't like chicarones, but she puts them in a paper bag for me. I walk out all excited, all proud, ready to give them to the first person I see, like a pilgrim passing on a piece of his cultural identity - his soul, his bones, his socks, the brown skin and bones that'll eventually be buried in a box. That's going to include my mama, his mama, him and me. And it just happens to be, it just works out to be, that the guy in front of me is sporting a Ricky Martin t-shirt, tight stonewashed jeans, and a bilingual mulette haircut. And I'm standing there thinking, that's just fine, that's just great, and I hand over that bag of chicarones real solemnly, like it's our first date.

I smile all mysterious like Theolonious Monk or something and say, "Hey man, these are from la cultura, la cultura." Thinking to myself while I'm looking at this guy, "Man, this is just holy as hell..." Shopping for la cultura don't always go down too well...

REAL LIFE CARTOON

I know, I know it's a re-run. Let me tell you anyways... Saturday morning in La Mission and already hogging a corner of 20th Street, los pinche placas and one of their undercover mustachoo muchacho gavacho got the local locos y locas down on baggy knees. Dangling their Ben Davis and virgen de Guadalupe t-shirts up against the laundromat wall where an abuelita blinks through the glass, holds her grandson's baptized hand and wonders if them socks are dry yet. While outside the mustachoo checks nicknames, belt buckles, shoelaces, and for a grand finale, lion tamer circus style, checks inside each and every one of those suereno sneers for any Tweetybird-size chiva balloons or Acme sticks of dynamite.

I know, I know it's a re-run but I watch anyways... Inhaling the smell of pan dulce from Jocelyn's across the street and waiting for an angel or an anvil to fall out of the sky. On top of all of this as the soundtrack's provided by the people gawking by, by the cars cruising by, slowing down with windows down hoping to get a better look at what's playing on the skin of those young brown arms and faces.

They know, they know, it's a re-run but they watch anyways... Hoping to get a look at some Tom cat and Jerry mouse, hoping to get a look at some cholos, fucking up el chavo del ocho's barrel house, hoping to get a look at that one chismosa, running to tell la chota something or other, azul y red rojo y blue.

Sometimes it's better than pay-per-view around here, chicano blood telenovelas staring at the kids that should be in las esquelas. Check your local listings or just look up the street from dropping dimes in Dolores Park to hanging out around Cesar Chavez Street after dark. You've met them before maybe on the way to the corner store or walking through when they was fighting for one more block of La Mission's territory. Speaking spanglish as they tell their story... senores y senoras no autographs please and no pictures either.

I know, I know it's a re-run and I know you already know... It's con safos on 24th y tu que? On 19th.

I know, I know it's a re-run but I told you anyways about Aztlan's violent children and their Looney Tune days.

CONTEMPLANDO LAS MOSCAS

Contemplando las moscas... and I got nothing to say on Thursday, at the bus stop after my blind date with La Llorona. She walks right in, man, and immediately starts crying on my shoulder even before the waiter came over with the sodas y wonton soup. There, am I right? Just thinking. *Please, oh please just don't start talking about your kids* is what I kept thinking. Through the mu shu vegetables y lemon chicken passing the time - man, I passed the time. Remember that old street nursery rhyme about that cholo que se volvio loco over that one ruca que se llamava Cuca after that poor cholo found out that Cuca already had some other vato's name tattooed in old English script on her ass.

Finally the #49 bus came and passed y La Llorona got on it and I slipped her my fortune cookie and my late-night transfer cuz there was no way I was taking anymore of that. I crossed the street onto 16th Street, passing the time remembering that other old street nursery rhyme about that one junkie juero in his prime. Living over there on lower Haight, he ended up living out of a suitcase milk crate, with not a thing in his room except a telephone, a radiator, and a spoon.

I guess sometimes it just works out that way, is what los dichos say, is what my abuelita would say, even if you ain't been doing nothing today except contemplando las moscas, and I still got nothing to say manana or the next day. Except got a stoner suspicion that gato negro of mine keeps stealing my breath away.

Oh yeah, my blue truck broke down by this wooden fence yesterday next to this real pretty garden statue of La Virgen de Guadalupe and I couldn't help it but for a couple of seconds there, walking over their lawn like that, tripping over their sprinklers like that, suddenly I felt just like Juan Diego with car trouble, no cigarettes y un jalle to get to and only a few plastic crosses from the Shell station to prove it all with. I got to ask since I'm here, Is this enough faith for what we're doing? Is this enough faith for what we done? In the meanwhile while that was going on, I figured out the latest thing you could do, the trendiest thing you can do, is take out a personal ad announcing to everybody just how bilingual you are.

"Living la Vida Loca" out of your car stereo and shit like that. Did you pick up all 2000 different versions of the Buena Vista Social Club yet, papi?

I don't mean to be cynical, but something always gets lost in translation - cuz of that ad, cuz of that fad, cuz of that phrase, that's just a phase and there you go, there you are too, walking around in Ben Davis that don't even fit. Worse still - looking around for a fashionable brown skin militant kind of chick cuz you hear that those types love to suck dick.

In this neighborhood are there any buildings to live in that still got murals on them? Y'know, maybe near them trendy bars, maybe not too far from some café - oh, hey, here's a good one - you got anything near Dolores Park? Is there anything affordable near Dolores Park anymore?

Pues es nada de mucho y es mucho de nada.

Where you going to go, mi junkie santa, where you going to go, mi otra mulatta? When all that's left of this is some expensive places to eat at, and some velvet paintings hanging next to some portraits of Willie Nelson, George W. Bush y el Last Supper, after the apocalypse has come and gone away and los prescriptions and subscriptions get cancelled on you anyways.

Pero, hey, in the meanwhile while that was going on, I swear, I swear, the Nescafe is still being poured on Sundays over there, and they slurp down menudo and soak up the culture with pan duro. While Flaco Jiminez keeps getting skinnier and the chupacabra just ate your dinner.

Te lo juro - it's true.

Te lo juro - it's true.

We may not look like it to you from over there but from over here under all of this we're just esceletos and we ain't been doing nothing today except *contemplando las moscas.*

Fuck you, I still got nothing to say, two weeks from today with two cups of coffee between us.

Something in her eye, something in my throat, something under the rug, and she finally gets around to asking that question that people always get around to asking you.... "Say man, say woman, say girl, say boy, what do you do anyways? What do you do anyways? What do you do anyways?"

Hay que la chingada this is the part I hate cuz hay que la chingada this is the part I can't really relate to. Sometimes I forget, sometimes I can't recall, sometimes virgen santa I swear I'm not trying to stall.

Just tell me who this is again - give me just a tiny hint por favor - is it any interviewer for life in general or what? Maybe mi cultura sent her cuz lately I been broke-assed out and funny looking cooking my last meal over and over again. She might be my old blond best friend and lover, the one whose brother is probably still looking to kick my ass up and down Valencia Street.

No, no, that's not it, that ain't right, now I remember: she was that vision I had back in September when I walked in fed up and ready to pawn it all, and she had a t-shirt with the feather red serpent on it. She said that not one lagrima would be shed for me, not one quetzal feather would fall to the earth for me, until I showed that serpenta what a pocho needed to be y despues de all of that.

After listening to all of this, that girl's still standing here. She's still praying for you, she lit a candle or two but she still wants to know, she's still curious to know, she still needs to know, "What do you do, anyways?"

That second time around all I can come up with, all I can say is, my eyes got a tendency to get cloudy out in the afternoon and if you want to know the truth chula, I don't understand things for a living. I'm trying real hard to read Horacio Quiroga in Spanish and I doorbell ditch houses, I T.P. houses in different languages for a living. On a buen dia I can vividly recall that look that Frida gives love and pain for a living, and for a while there I kept coming back to my old neighborhood trying to separate mi sangre from the rain for a living.

That rain that would drip off them Spanish-speaking pigeons, them used syringes that faded confetti left over from some nina's quinceniera wishes and anybody who's lived around here has met a dealer named Lalo for a living, baby, and anybody who's lived around here has had pan dulce on Sunday morning for a living, and anybody who's lived around here has done their laundry at the laundromat for a living, and I don't know why I can't explain it but me gusta that way. I've gotten used to it being that way, like I said me gusta that way, like looking right through an aquarium on a real good day and damn if I ain't done nothing today except

Contemplando las moscas....
Contemplando las moscas....
Contemplando las moscas....

DON MIGUEL

don miguel's worked 9733 lunch shifts and over 10,000 dinner shifts in the time that i've known him.

yeah don miguel knows what's going on
from the kitchen sink to michoacán
yeah don miguel knows what's going on
from the kitchen sink to michoacán...

he got crushed up baby aspirin and birth control pills, para las flores that don't grow, and he got cigar smoke for whatever comes out at night and a curandero over in los angeles that he's been going to for years whenever the young ladies go and give him the shakity shakes

yeah don miguel knows what's going on
from the kitchen sink to michoacán
yeah don miguel knows what's going on
from the kitchen sink to michoacán...

he always eats back there standing up just looking at the silverware that's drying back there and scooping up everything on his plate with a tortilla while the faucets drip and the pots boil and the fryers fry don miguel's got tiny eyeballs stuffed

full with miles and miles slickback jetblack hairstyles and a
smooth profile taken right off a bullfighting velvet painting, a
brown forehead full of sayings that'll probably take me years
to really figure out and even if the devil were burning his feet
he'd still wave buenos dias to you

>   yeah don miguel knows what going on
>   from the kitchen sink to michoacán
>   yeah don miguel knows what going on
>   from the kitchen sink to michoacán...

don miguel he speaks the language, he's just calling it all by an
older name, he can mumble in bilingual and laughs without
bothering anyone but you know they can hear him, you know
they seen him, he's been from here to there and back again,
he's been from there to heremand back across the border again
again and againmand y' know even from all that, don miguel
never looks rushed - he's always on time, he never rides that
overcrowded bus, you always see him walking down 4th street
with his head held high like paul bunyan, like john henry, like
don quixote, like pancho villa, like zapata, like chewbacca

>   yeah don miguel knows what's going on
>   from the kitchen sink to michoacán
>   yeah don miguel knows what's going on
>   from the kitchen sink to michoacán...

FLOWER AND SONG EACH AND EVERY DAY

Simone pues, it was el Dia de Los Muertos and we were in
the procesion drifting along with all the monos and the locos
and them everyday smells that normally don't go together,
simmering and flavoring that autumn weather. Carne asada
and candle wax drifting past las familias watching it all in front
of Bryant Street railroad flats - las candelas tonight dripping
for dead ninos amigos grandmas y primos who have gone on
and on and on but for tonight are allowed back.

They are allowed to stand right next to the manic panic
dyed hairs and urban street wears who stop and stare at los
esceletos in the street doing their sugarskull jigs right next to
the Halloween costumes that have been on since Sunday. It

started with dancing in the streets of the Castro, then freaking up and down Market Street all the way to Monday. Now I'm home, I'm walking through home, I'm part of my home in some way and one of the old, old cuentos from back in the day says that one time the quetzal prince woke up in a fright in the middle of the night and went to his favorite philosopher with the question, "Hey you, how best is truth spoken?"

Supposedly that philosopher answered him quit simply, "My prince, a flower and song is the original token."

Floricanto es la verdad.

It was an Aztec who predicted that... or did I read it scrawled on the bathroom wall over at Dr. Bombay's? Even though I forget, I got to try real hard to remember a flower and song each and every day.

Simone pues, well, it was el Dia de Los Muertos and we were in the procession drifting along with the freaky musical selection, you had a couple of drunk mariachi bands, a ranchera band, a hippie with a conch shell, hippie with a djemba, some plastic tubes tied to bones. Some guy playing a homemade paper saxophone, and we pass by a guy on the payphone, screaming above the noise talking to la muerte, telling la peluda how he's all alone, it can't be over yet, please don't let it be over yet.

We take a right on 25th, pass some vatos sharing a fifth of vodka and smiling at it all in Spanish while the leftover jack-o-lanterns behind them got carved up in English, and now I'm home, I'm walking through home, I'm part of my home in some way.

Supposedly that old old cuento from back in the day continues like this, that quetzal prince didn't like the answer his favorite philosopher gave him so he put on his feathered cloak and sandals got in his SUV and drove down to the avenue of the dead where all the young nahuals sold their dope and copped and coped with life under the fifth sun and the queztal prince asked each and ever one of them, "Children, how best is truth spoken?" One by one by one they all answered, "My prince, a flower and song is the original token."

Floricanto es la verdad.

Now, did I inherit that truth from mi abuelo or overhear it from a Tenderloin bum in a torn orange sweater? Even though I forget, I got to try real hard to remember.

A flower and song each and every day.

Simone pues, well, it was el dia de los muertos and we were in the procession surrounded by all these worldly possessions, walking by the parking meters, the store windows. The concrete underneath our feet that'll outlast all of our bones and this baby carriage goes drifting by filled with corn and dry ice and smoking with sage, and I bump into my buddy Angel from back in the old days, still living in Oakland and playing accordion. And right next to him is a couple of bearded nuns, right next to them is some cute girl with tinfoil dreads, and right next to this group of cholos is my friend Justin, who is dead. He got taken out of life a few years back by being stabbed by a boy so tonight I get to light him a cigarette and remember his joy.

And there goes Toby, still acting like he don't know me, and here comes my mama grande who's been dead ten years since Sunday. Now I'm home, I'm walking through home, I'm part of my home in some way. Supposedly that old old cuento from back in the day keeps on going and going until eventually the quetzal prince is going to catch up to the modern man and ask him, "Hey, modern man, how best is truth spoken?" And hopefully the modern man will answer, "My prince, a flower and song is the original token."

Floricanto es la verdad

Now did some indigenous pachuco hero steal that truth from a god or did I read it on a decal on some cholos hot rod? Even though I forget I got to try real hard to remember, a flower and song each and every day....

NOPAL BLUES

El amor de un nopal
es muy dificil tocar

y cuando todo hay pasado
y tienes en tus bracos eso nopal abrasado

vas a ver
como te va picar y picar y picar

hasta que al fin vas a griatar
??hay Diosito santo
que estab pensando??
esos piqeticos
me estan matando...

pero toda via segues abrasando
esos nopalitos que teo siguen picando...

The love of a cactus
is very difficult to touch

but after everything is said and done
and at last you have in your arms that cactus

you're going to see
how it pricks you and pricks and pricks

until at last you're going to scream
oh my God
what was I thinking??
these little pinpricks
are killing me...

but I still keep on hugging
the cactus that keeps piercing me...

DANI MONTGOMERY is a queer activist, teacher, and poet who grew up in Tucson and San Diego. She has taught poetry with June Jordan's Poetry for the People and San Francisco WritersCorps. Her poems have appeared in *the Santa Clara Review*, *Anything That Moves*, *Icarus* and other magazines.

DEAR BROTHER

your picture's propped up on my dresser
cloudy gray eyes and perpetually messed up hair
above a half sarcastic smile.
you defended me throughout our childhood:
against our mother
against our father
against all the kids in the neighborhood—
you'd come home with a ripped shirt
broken bone
black eye
and say it was nothing,
nothing,
don't worry about it.

so I know when the recruiter calls you
like so many other high school seniors
you want to answer yes
because you want to protect somebody
you don't want mom to feel shamed
for what she can't pay for
so you say you'll enlist
be a proud third generation soldier
or you'll take an ROTC college scholarship
if you can get it
promising eight years of service
for four years of tuition.
and you probably
secretly
feel proud you'll be
protecting your country

imagine yourself evacuating americans
from some conflict driven region
or helping refugees across a river.

baby brother
every night I go to sleep with those eyes
comforting me from my dresser
and I don't want an afghani daughter
to wake up in terror to those same eyes
i don't want an eighteen-year-old iraqi soldier's
plans for college and career
erased by the path of a missile you launched
because brother
the FBI doesn't monitor our family
for deadly kitchen conversation
you don't get pulled off planes
for having blond hair and a southern california accent
but you / but we
have to consider
who's the real terrorist risk here?

we argue and argue
til you clench your jaw and look away
i know you well enough to read
i gotta do what I gotta do
in the set of your lips
but I can't get that afghani girl
out of my head
every day I open the paper
read the latest atrocities
and imagine what it will be like
to read the regiment number
and find
that was my baby brother
who burned that village
yes, my brother
arrested all the young men in town
and sent them to barbed wire ringed
detention camps,
yes, my brother did that.

i imagine reading
marine killed in conflict
and staying up all night by the phone
praying for it not to ring
that terrible, final
ring.

i can't call george w.
and tell him what I think of his genocidal schemes
i can't get rumsfeld or ashcroft on the phone
to say don't play young boys' lives like poker chips
i can't knock on sharon's door and ask
when he'll be leaving palestine
but I can ask you
to reconsider participating in their plans.
brother
you've gotta do what you've gotta do
and I respect that
but I pray you'll choose to find any other way
because these choices
are what we have to fight back with
because
you have the most gorgeous gray eyes i've ever seen
but that beauty
depends on whose looking and when
because your wanting to do right
doesn't mean you won't do wrong
i'm begging you
baby brother
please reconsider.

WHAT I REMEMBER MOST ABOUT THE HARD TIMES

the woman who opened a produce store
in the mini mall on jackson
who let us have groceries on credit
and once

when my distracted mother
left the prized bag on the counter
we arrived home to find it on the porch
an extra head of lettuce peeking out the top;

the neighbor who was equally broke as us
who brought by a box of
top ramen and rice and pasta n sauce,
the neighbor who gave me
five bucks when she had it
and a hug when she didn't;

the cashier at the corner burrito shop
who let my mother and brother order whatever they wanted
and pay whatever they had;

all the checkers who didn't laugh
when I paid with a plastic bag of pennies
who just smiled and helped me count
even when the line of people with places to go
started to sigh in stereo.

this is what I remember most about the hard times:
the people who helped us because they'd worn
that same nervous smile on their own faces
the ones who knew what it was like to stand there
rooting through your pockets
making up explanations.

CODED
(for my mother and everyone else who's lived on the streets)

i pass a woman
asleep in an avenue doorway
and I think she looks like my mother
something about the slope of her shoulders
the tangle of dark brown hair
tossed over her navy bedroll

for a moment it is thirty years ago
and this is my mother
dirty fingernails clutching at her forearms
as she tries to block the cold breath of morning
my mother
reaching into her sleeping bag
for her paper swaddled bottle of wine
my mother
rubbing oozing eyes that refuse to open
stuck fast against the thin razors of light

i can almost remember
the way wine burns the throat
heat panging away against so much cold
seeping into thin anemic blood
and I taste iron
i can feel the blistered corners
of her mouth split as she repeats:
spare change sir spare change ma'am
spare change
spare change
like an old song
the words vibrate against my cheeks

i wonder if memory is coded into our cells
shards of the past in our hair in our fingernails
in these moments when we can see
the ash gray sky at six a.m.
on a morning when we were only pin dots
buried in the folds of some woman's abdomen
i whisper *I love you*
to the lady in the doorway
and continue down the avenue
warming my numb red hands
against the growing fire of sunrise

BUTCH FEMME EAST COUNTY LOVE POEM

you can be the hero of my country song
drive up in your truck
and take me for a ride
c'mon
you can buy me beers
i'll buy you tequila shots
you can open the door for me
i'll wear that black skirt you like
you can slide your hand
up my thigh in the diner
i can feed you orange slices in bed
you can bite that soft spot behind my left ear
i can make you scream
like you swore you wouldn't
you can feel free
to leave marks across my ass

we can piss my whole family off
making out on easter morning
we can send your dad off hunting
and your mom to bed with a headache
by just showing up

i can bind your breasts
clip the ace bandage
so the pins won't stick
i can kiss your nipples hard
when you release them

you can hold my hand
when cops spit at us
i can hold your hand
when men swear at us
i can wield a knife
you can throw some mean punches
we can go down with a hell of a fight
if we have to

you can sing me alan jackson
i can sing you willie nelson
we can turn the radio up
and laugh about all those times
our folks were broke

i can smoke
and you can tell me not to
i can love the way you wear your jeans
you can love how I sweat
through the armpits of all my dresses
you can wash the dishes
i can forget to do the laundry
you can teach me how to shoot
i can teach you to steal and not get caught
you can bring me daisies
i'll bring you gardenias

c'mon let's go
i know the words already
you gotta help me sing

BROKEN BACKS
(after hearing tiny's poem *my broken back*)

I.
at fifty-four
my mother has a hard time
getting around the block.
each step makes her jaw pop—
she clamps her teeth together
and sucks in a hard breath.

the doctor says
it was so many years
of carrying heavy things:
children, boxes, beds,
whatever had to be moved
she lifted on her hip or

heaved over her shoulder
and got where it needed to go.

the doctor shows her the x-ray:
two vertebrae crushed against each other.
the only way to fix it?
replace part of her spine with plastic.
she tells him she'll be fine.

II.
my mother taught me to laugh when it hurts
and never need help
and because of that
i have survived.
but sometimes these muscles rebel:
i end up in bed
unable to move for days
fading in and out of
a cyclobenzaprine haze

she calls and asks how i'm doing.
i say *fine*.
except I threw my back out.
she sighs, tells me
that's how it starts.
none of the pills will help,
you really need to do less, to rest.
but you probably won't, will you, she says.
i know just how you are.

A LOVE POEM FOR WALT WHITMAN

our america sits on corners
jangling change in cups
blisters her fingers on stove coils
in cafeteria kitchens
scrubs the speckled linoleum
of school bathrooms at ten p.m.

our america wears scuffed flats
with goodwill blouses
and answers phones all day
rents cars with insurance
for a low low price
stands behind counters
and slides credit cards through cash registers
our america tricks on the boulevard
sells ziploc bags of weed up the block
packs groceries   pumps gas
stitches polo shirts together in jail

our america
gets up each morning
even though today she may be arrested
and he may be deported
even though she can't afford the rent
and he can't pay to see a doctor
even though death hovers low on the horizon
our america continues
to insist on itself
and with every morning
rises

MY LAST ANSWER TO
"CAN I ASK YOU A PERSONAL QUESTION?"
(to everyone who is upset and/or fascinated by my lover's
transition from female to male)

this is what I know:
when I lie next to him
in between our eyelet-edged sheets
(the ones he picked out)
his belly skin brushes smooth sanded
soft against mine his
hands are work scarred and
perfectly textured playing
with the contours of my hip bones
and I am not at all concerned

with whether you think me
a traitor
for loving this man
i began loving as a woman
or consider me a freak
for wanting every last inch of him
as he is
and as he
is not.

it doesn't even cross my mind
to worry if you
hate   or   pity
this brilliance

i am lost in calculation of
how many kisses can fit
across the field of his palm
i am deep in a meditation of
eyelashes and earlobes
i am consumed
by the continuing path of his hands
around my hips by his
still startled exhale at my
evident desire

this means nothing more than love
nothing less than defiance and
you can theorize it
impossible
but you will be finally
gloriously
            incorrect.

A QUESTION TO THE GUARDS AT
JUVENILE HALL

how do you go home in the evening and

hold your baby
touch your lover
cook food

with the same hands
that this afternoon
fastened shackles
around the wrists
of a fifteen-year-old girl?

DUBLIN SNAPSHOTS:
A VISIT TO KILMAINHAM JAIL

rise to birth with me my brother
give me your hand out of the depths
sown by your sorrows...
speak through my speech,
and through my blood.
                    —*Pablo Neruda*

1. the road to the jail

a woman sells oranges and dusty bottles of soap
from a leaning card table on the corner
her eyes cupped by dark moons,
her hair split and thick with oil,
her red feet swelling out the tops of her canvas shoes.

i want to know the story
of each crease in her forehead
the huge knots of her joints
the bruises wrapping her arms.
i want to ask:

what stars peeked in on your arrival?
what stories did your mother plant in the coil of your ear,
what did you watch for out the kitchen window
sunday afternoons?

what do you imagine now
as trucks spit gravel in your face
and exhaust slides down your throat,
what ache has burrowed there
between your jutting breast bones?

2. kilmainham jail

these walls breathe in the cold
and exhale warmth out their windows
in the doorframe of each cell
name after name
has been dug in jagged strokes

each letter hints at an entire life:
a girl who made up songs about bees
a man who laughed like a ship's horn
soldiers who fought for a revolution
of grain and land and the sound of their own language.

this one hanged in the square
this one shot in the exercise yard
the others burnt by a fever
halfway across the atlantic.

their unspoken testimony
makes the wet air
heavy

3. walking away

boarded up windows of projects
line the road like shut eyes.
downtown there are fresh bricked roads
new statues

an army of men in blue suits
who shake hands furiously.

here there is the dirt-stained glass
of abandoned storefronts,
a sour smell climbing from sewers,
the prison hulking in the background.
the revolution was a long time ago.

a mother holds her toddler's hand
as they cross slow at the light—
a step across the asphalt
then another
then one more.

AT THE PEACE WALL
(belfast, northern ireland, two years after the good friday agreement)

mary stands guard on the lawn
her plaster face worn with the stress of years.
this house is a miracle:
its sides freckled with bullet holes
its roof scorched and patched.

you could reach out the back window
and touch the cold steel of the peace wall.
teenagers yell taunts from the other side
oh danny boy, hey danny boy

nights molotov cocktails shriek over the razor wire
hurled by unseen hands.
mornings the kids brush their teeth
and eat cold cereal in the kitchen.

this is the ordinariness of war:
a mother sweeps broken glass off the pavement
calling *be careful* as her children march to school.

STILL HOLDING

this year is
dried mango slices from safeway and
popeye's biscuits,
two for ninety-two cents,
when we're studying early in the morning.

this year's a speech that has to get written
for a conference tomorrow,
an essay for an application due today,
a poem that must come together in the next fifteen
minutes.

this year
is nachos from the store downstairs
with burnt weak coffee in a styrofoam cup
when class goes way past dinner
and you didn't get lunch.
this year drinks gallons of alka-seltzer and licorice root tea
and wishes for a calm stomach.

this year has way too much to do
and not enough to do it with and
it's nearly impossible
to pay the bills,
deal with today's news,
and get to work each day.
it's even harder to sit at that table
monday nights and write—
harder still
to convince yourself
someone will listen.

this year needs hershey's kisses by the handful
and those stale red vines you buy five at a time
in a thin brown paper bag.
this year
will eat anything sweet you offer.

this year is a poem you don't think is any good
but when you read it
your voice shakes us awake
makes us remember why we brave
the rain and the always late bus and
all the everyday catastrophes
to get here.

a poem that promises:
you don't know
where you'll stay tonight
but you'll be here tomorrow.
a poem that hopes
enough people show up
to tomorrow's demonstration
that the officials
behind their mahogany rail realize
finally
we matter.
a poem that prays
please don't send our sister
to prison
please let my brother
lying in intensive care
live
please stretch this last dollar
long enough
to get us all home.

a poem about
how your tired hand still holds that pen
a poem about
    how your throat is raw but your voice still carries
a poem about how your strength
still holds.

GHAZAL FOR THE DUENDE OR
HOW I BECAME A POET

you might be hiding something sharp inside the doctor says
she closes her eyes while the guard checks her underwear

there is a fountain in the courtyard outside the asylum
she presses her ear to the concrete and listens for falling water

all night the boy strapped to the wall in solitary howls
she dreams the seamless plastic window opens and she steps
   onto god's hand

even here her scarred arms are fascinating
the nurses say *keep your sleeves pulled up so we can see*

when they find her wedged between the bed and the wall
   she starts screaming
like the devil got stuck in her throat—she hasn't ever stopped

POEM TO MY LANDLORD

i got paid last week
but my bank account still claims it's overdrawn.

i tried every credit card
but each one came up denied.

i considered another trip to the pawn shop
but none of my stuff would sell.

i contemplated placing an ad for a sugar daddy
but my lover struck down that idea.

so instead of sending rent
i sat down to write:
i hope you will accept this poem
in lieu of monetary payment.

it's a sound investment
on your part
when i'm a famous poet
you can auction it off
or mount it above your mantel
to make your friends jealous.
really
call your broker
ask him how much
genuine
poetry
is worth in this market
i'm sure
he won't even be able
to calculate that much.

POEM ABOUT MY PENIS
(because some people will not shut up about theirs)

i don't mean to brag, but
mine comes in several sizes
different diameters
with glitter or ridges
and I can even
leave it at home.

BAD BREAKUP

the phantom scent of beer follows me
finds me walking down mission street,
standing in front of my building,
waiting for an outbound train.

instead of sex
i dream of gin bottles
clinking their curves together,
i dream my hands on the hips
of a vodka bottle.

liquor is such a bad lover
but I can't seem to let her go.

in the morning I feel disgusted with us both
but by noon i'm infatuated again.
i said
maybe if we don't see each other so often
i said
let's be friends
i said
we can dance at parties
go to dinner occasionally
and that's it.
but I ignore all my resolutions
by the second drink,
forget them by the fourth,
and after that
i'm completely positive
it's true love.

i've quit drinking again
and now i'm not nearly as popular.
most of our friends were really hers.
there's no way to avoid her—
if I go out, she's already there,
standing by the bar
sparkling in the dim light.
and I don't like to be rude
so i'll go over to say hi,
but it never ends there.

in an instant
we're lip to lip again
with me begging
baby come home with me
this time I won't get distracted
you can consume me piece by piece
first my stomach
then my liver
finally   my heart.

but i've quit drinking
again.
my muscles layer themselves into sediment
beneath my skin.
at night I grind my molars into fine sand.
i wake up crying
chanting
this will be the last time
the last the last   the last
this has to be the last time.
i have got to let her go.

WHAT IS LEFT

i punch my time card
and walk into monday night's chill
as the train lumbers past
its rusted steel clanging and lurching
with the pressure of so much speed
it heaves out a staccato whistle and continues on
down the dark corridor of warehouses
their windows patched with plywood
their long abandoned doorways sagging

across the tracks
a bonfire spits and cracks with heat
two men crouch against a concrete wall
and warm their bodies over the flame
feeding it scraps of wood and paper
as the wind gusts they pull in closer
a human knot around
the only light left for miles

JAMES TRACY is a long-time organizer active in anti-poverty work. He is coordinator of Right to a Roof, a part of San Francisco's Coalition on Homelessness. He is also the author of *The Civil Disobedience Handbook: A Brief History and Practical Advice for the Politically Disenchanted* (Manic D Press) and *The Donut Hole* (Kapow Books).

PRESSURE

in the front of the same cafe
day after day

"no pressure, give if you can"
"no pressure, give if you can"
"no pressure, give if you can"

jessie, he was the no pressure man

if you put a rattle in his can
he said thank you then
thank you again

if you walked on by
he said
see you next time

with the kind of smile that said
i'm gonna die with this smile
and you will die
with all your things
clenched close to your heart

but that's o.k.

"no pressure, give if you can"
"no pressure, give if you can"
"no pressure, give if you can"

stop and talk and he might

tell you about
the south he moved north from
maybe vietnam

or his ex-wife constance
and alphonse her old man
who might come around the corner
for another rematch

because stakes are high
with any game with the word
love in it

they'd go at it again
like ali and foreman

but it was all about no pressure
even when the ranks of the
spare change samaritans
got unbearable for that small businessman

even as the parade of
perfect lattes
passed him by like
ellison's invisible man

never any pressure
as the rich built and bought castles
around him

no pressure as valet parking
took people around the cafe
altogether

no pressure
as all the demonstrations
and mobilizations
went right on by

no pressure as the niños

went to college, prison or
straight to work
after high school

no pressure
when the twenty-somethings
became thirty-somethings
and talk of the record deal became
talk of when we were kings

no pressure
as they built a new police station
right down the block
in the old pepsi-cola bottling company

then one day his milk crate
was there
and on that day
his spare change cup was there

but jessie wasn't there
anymore

plastic flowers
laid there in his place

i am told he finally got tired of
so much
pressure

NEW WORLD ORDERS

Remember these things to survive interesting times:

1) All phones are tapped so make every word you say count.

2) Everything you say has already been used against you, so
speak boldly anyhow.

3) All current governments are terrorist states.

4) There are two kinds of terrorist states: those who come to the table smoking a cigar and those who come to the table bringing spare-change cups; nonetheless both are terrorist states.

5) Ecological Capitalism is an oxymoron. The only thing that is ever truly recycled is Manifest Destiny.

6) Since the South Pole is really the top of the world it makes it easier to hold developing countries by their bootstraps and shake the last coin from them.

7) Prisons are the new social/public housing.

8) Pictures of Che Guevara sell records.

9) The Right Wing is under the illusion that there is such a thing called a free market.

10) Many Progressives are under the illusion that there is such a thing as a free lunch.

11) Patriotism means never having to say "I'm sorry."

12) If Rudolph Guiliani becomes president, then sodomy with a plunger at the hands of the police will become a sacrament.

13) If most Americans have to ask "Why does the world hate us?" then we may already be doomed.

14) Homelessness has become a new rite of passage for the working class.

15) If voting could change the world, it would be outlawed, but if it were completely ineffective, George Bush wouldn't have had to steal the election in Florida.

THE POLITICAL ECONOMY OF
TEACHING CLASS

Each day you write instructions about what it takes to
survive in a world like this,
guerilla street corner capitalism and
county jailhouse justice.

When you can't even make it back from lunch
without being stopped by the police,
how am I supposed to get up in front of class and say,
with a straight face that the U.S. Constitution provides us all
with certain inalienable rights ?

At this school, poetry is spoken
sometimes without the speakers knowing it:
Ebonics meets the Manong,
Spanglish arrests the Queen's English.

The school always finds its teacher, even at 3 a.m. my phone rings-

A student demands an audience for a piece about how
one more strike and he's out
and life's not a ballgame so don't try to play me,
"What will happen to the fiancée and the baby?"
He says, "Hey teacher! Put my poem up on the wall,
so if I do more years than Mumia Abu Jamal
at least there's proof I got my education."

What he really wants to know is
if he has proper grammatical form
and are we literate yet ?

"Can you write a letter about my character and send it c/o my p.o.?"

I go back to sleep afraid that there is no judge or jury
soft for ghetto poets and housing project prophets.
How do you explain the political economy of a city that
doesn't want its children anymore ?

Instead of homework she brings in an eviction notice and
there's hardly anything they teach you in college
that prepares you for days like these.

Every Friday three-fifteen the words of the ascended, most wise
Saint Tupac Shakur of the Church of the
Could of,
Should of,
Might Have Been
ring out...
"Keep your head up," leads into
"Later, teacher, have a good weekend and
don't let the bullshit get you down."

ANTI-WAR TEACH-IN AT THE VETERANS'
ADMINISTRATION HOSPITAL

Universities out
of anti-war teach-ins, now !

Academies out
of anti-war teach-ins, now !

This anti-war teach-in
is at the Veterans' Administration Hospital.

In Room 104...
John Johnson
A man whose addiction
shot a Ho Chi Mihn trail
through his body.

Heroin was the only thing
that could beat the pangs
of Manifest Destiny from him
Room 127...
Raphael Franklin Gonzalez
There's a phantom itch
where his leg used to be.

In the courtyard...
The Unknown Soldier sits in
a wheelchair and screams the screams
that should be heard around the world.

A TALE OF TWO GIULIANIS

A year ago we hurled our poetry up against the wall of the San Francisco Italian Consulate. We threw accusations and exhortations *"assessinos, asessinos, assessinos"* against an old white facade.

They were dancing in memory of Carlo Giuliani. Some were singing in memory of Carlo Giuliani. Others were screaming in memory of Carlo Giuliani.

A young Italian murdered in the streets of Genoa by the Italian police since he would not let them stop the shutdown of misery as usual and the growth of the young movement. We reminded the crowd that in between here and Italy was Fourth and Mission where the San Francisco police had emptied dozens of bullets into a young Idriss Stelley, an unarmed young man whose every day was a struggle as sure as any waged in the streets for just a little piece of sanity.

There is another Giuliani, Rudolph Giuliani. He thought that Abner Luima and Amadou Diallo had it coming, and most Italian-Americans didn't blink an eye, even if that had happened to one of our own there would have been a riot in Little Italy. In America, we the Italians, have forgotten what it means to stand for the downtrodden.

We can't even remember that, yes, the Italians were interned in World War II. Amnesia makes silence easier if it is someone else's face behind the bars, someone else's face at the bottom of the well, someone else's body under the nightstick, someone else's family running from immigration, someone else's rectum raped with a plunger.

It is just the price you pay when you're writing overdrawn checks on the wages of whiteness.

Did my great-grandmother Nonni ever light candles for Sacco and Vanzetti?

Or was she too busy working in the New World to notice what was happening? Was she too busy cleaning offices in the New World to notice what was happening?

Carlo Guiliani had another world in his heart.

Rudolph Guiliani has blood on his hands.

Carlo Guiliani lay in a pool of blood.

Rudolph Guiliani makes millions of dollars speaking about leadership.

Carlo Guiliani's impatience for a better world broke windows.

Rudolph Guiliani speaks with a forked tongue.

Carlo Guiliani spoke through the deed.

Rudolph Guiliani unleashed an army upon the heads of the homeless.

Carlo Guiliani unleashed his fury upon glass of an armor tank carrier.

Today, Rudolph Guiliani's vision of the future has its hands around the neck of the future

Carlo Guiliani wanted to live in.

GRANDFATHER'S HANDS

I presented the life of a young radical to my grandfather late one night in his mobile home in the foothills. He asked how I spent my days and I answered that I helped public housing residents who were organizing against the government demolishing their homes. We organized a rally in Civic Center and how we would make a movement bigger than any of the buildings.

Point blank he shot, "Serves the niggers right, they trashed those places as soon as they moved in. I'm glad they are finally tearing those dumps down." He sipped a glass of water and said, "Don't waste your time, son, you don't have anything to feel guilty about."

Any rhetoric I had about red-lining, and race, class and cops couldn't help us understand each other that night.

"I would tear those buildings down with my own hands if I could," he mumbled. I tried to change the subject to the days we used to fish together and how he taught me to stand in his tiny fiberglass boat pissing into Collins Lake. The previous four years were strung together by my broken promises to come up and fish together so those words wouldn't build a bridge between us either.

He then talked about being the son of immigrants and working with your hands. He talked about carrying a bullet in his stomach for thirty years. He talked about how he was forced to load trucks at gunpoint during the 1946 General Strike while his union boss looked on.

He talked about how the Irish would treat the Italians like shit. How he believed that America was still very beautiful. Anyone could get a little something here if they worked hard and appreciated what they had.

We sat in the dark and listened to the crickets.
We went to bed without coming to conclusions.
We woke up and made a big breakfast.

When I left he hugged me with his strong Teamster hands; the same hands that held me when I was young. Those were the same hands that made me feel like the safest child alive. As I drove to San Francisco I thought that I couldn't believe that those kind hands would volunteer to tear anyone's home down.

SOME OF OUR BEST FRIENDS ARE CANNIBALS

we would never object
to their hiring and promotion
you see
some of our best friends are cannibals!
although we secretly hope they don't
want to date our daughters
we want you to know
some of our best friends are cannibals!
it was hard however to have them
over for dinner their feelings were
hurt because they thought we would
fix them a vegetarian
instead of a vegetarian meal
we realize that hannibal lector

is a cruel stereotype used to
oppress the cannibals,
we don't even really like
the word cannibal we prefer
flesh-eating american
we understand cannibals,
we think they have a taste
for what it really means to be human.
some of our best friends are cannibals!
we understand the cannibals
because we are.

A MILLION REVOLUTIONS

walking in circles, I picket myself
do not patronize! self unfair to self and others

boycotting myself like a field strawberry
i will not buy my own bullshit anymore

leading a sit-down strike in my own room
until better living conditions are achieved

washing my molotov mouth out with soap
for kinder, gentler dialogue

stepping outside and smiling
the earth moves a million revolutions per minute

QUEEN SALMON

You have been away from the world for five years now.
You have been away from
viruses and rumors of viruses,
rent hikes and queer bashings
for five years now.

Your ashes remained in a box;

kept next to
record collections and oil paintings
televisions and boom boxes.

You made so much drama and
borrowed so much money in life that
we assumed you might try to at least
keep us safe from the comfort of your afterworld.

You got credit for the twin towers of
Joe and Becca Giera surviving
a catastrophic car crash since your ashes
were in the back of their now-twisted truck.

We now take those ashes atop a small log bridge
above Prairie Creek and dump you in
with a few kind words and intelligent guesses
about how punk rock queens are treated in the hereafter.
In the name of the Great Mother Earth
and the pursuit of the perfect gig.

In the name of our holy trinity
Joey Ramone,
Wendy O Williams
and Marianne Anderson.

In the presence of ancient redwoods,
elk herds,
and ancient forests.

In the land Judi Bari fought for
your ashes fall from the bridge and
wind like a long stripe that
will arrive at the Pacific Ocean in an hour.

A lone giant salmon treads upstream,
tracing your trail,
fighting the current like you fought
just about everything.

BUSH II

Bush who?
Bush two!
Bush who?
Bush two!

King George the Second
Rumored prophesized by Nostradamus
as the village idiot
sings an executioner's song.
The Hangman of Texas
wouldn't be sad if
Rosa Parks herself died
of a lethal injection.

Bush who?
Bush two!
Bush who?
Bush two!

Nick Nack Paddy Wack...
He bombed Iraq
as soon as he took the oath,
This George Bush is natural born.
(Killer, that is.)

Bush who?
Bush two!
Bush who?
Bush two!

His empire is of oil and gold,
and nuclear power so we all can glow.
He brings back Star Wars!
His Empire Takes Back!
He is Close Encounters of a Bell Curve Unkind!

Bush who?
Bush two!

Bush who?
Bush two!

We pledge allegiance...
    to the United States of Virtual Unreality
We pledge allegiance...
    to the Republic of Shopping Carts
We pledge allegiance...
    to the home of oh hell(th) care
We pledge allegiance...
    to forced sterilization
We pledge allegiance...
    to forced breeding
We pledge allegiance...
    to McPrisons
We pledge allegiance...
    to McMedicare
We pledge allegiance...
    to we didn't know it was just a wallet
We pledge allegiance...
    to the food stamp vanishing like the last great buffalo

Bush who?

WEN HO LEE

Wen Ho Lee,
a man who knows how to destroy the world
sits shackled in solitary
for downloading the final solution
into the wrong computer
at Los Alamos
the town which
may bring us doomsday
has more to answer for
than Wen Ho Lee

The United States of Anxiety
sleeps fitfully with nightmares
of a new red threat

If Wen Ho Lee isn't made to suffer
hoards of Chinese Maoists
will certainly march through
Main Street teaching everyone
"Love and serve the people"

The Red Army will catch
Julia Roberts and make her more
Brokovitch than Pretty Woman

Why is it that Americans are afraid of the Chinese?
China is granted favored trade status and
runs neck in neck with the U.S. in
incarceration for fun and profit

The only yellow peril we have to fear is the earth burning
brighter than a thousand jaundiced suns
thanks to the fruit of Los Alamos

We hear Joe McCarthy
 "Are you now or have you ever been—
a Mickey Maus citizen ?"

Are enemies created because they are needed?
Only the Rosenberg ghosts and the slaughtered students of
Tiananmen Square know for sure.

YOU CAN GET IT FROM

You can get it from
thinking bad thoughts and
touching yourself or
not touching anything at all.

You can get it from
giving a cop the bird and
writing your name on the wall or
writing someone else's name on a stall.
You can get it from

not paying your taxes
lying to your lover or
lying with your lover.

You can get it from
voting for the lesser of two evils and
not voting for the lesser of two evils or
yelling fire in a crowded theater.

You can get it from
drinking milk left out all night and
not washing behind the ears or
leaving dirt underneath your fingernails.

You can get it from
eating very mad cows and
drinking soy milk or
eating out of a dumpster.

You can get it from
laughing at racist jokes and
being politically correct
or never being correct about anything.

You can get it from
driving while black and
driving while brown or
driving over state lines with lustful intent.

You can get it from
running for the border and
running for office or
standing still in perfect silence.

You can get it from
dancing in the soup line and
screaming at the symphony or
betting on a one trick pony again and again and again.

LIFE AFTER

We walk, miles strong through the streets of Porto Alegre, Brazil. The world's languages fly into the air and dance like butterflies in courtship; or the Tower of Babel reconstructing itself from the ground up. This is the country of the movements of landless workers. A country of cautious hope now - Brazil is in a dance; not a tango or an easy two-step, more like Capoeria.

A graceful swing could kick the system in the cajones, or throw the country of Paulo Freire into a death stumble. The ghost of Allende, the specter of Pinochet are everywhere here.

Red flags! Black flags! Red and Black flags!

Walking past the Gigantino Stadium, it is easy to get drunk on all of this. It tastes exactly unlike the drink we usually sip; too easy to think that revolution is already won instead of always running.

Too easy to fool oneself that all we have to do is walk backwards. Backwards from a glorious future until today; I let myself believe that war is no more since this war doesn't exist on the faces around me. Zapatistas take off their masks and share their smiles with the world. Lungs are filled with song fueled by clean oxygen, not screams fueled by crack cocaine or the juice of toxic racism.

Israel and Palestine just worked it out. The WTO, the IMF, the SOA, the FBI went out of business.

Segregation is confined to a strict separation between cockroaches and people in the former slums, shantytowns and projects. Work as we knew it ended until work becomes more like play until work becomes the task of rebuilding the broken world.

The big strike has been extended indefinitely to give everyone a chance to rest from too many long hours. A retroactive weekend!

The only intelligence agent we'll need is having the intelligence to know that the annual rituals of assassination, economic sabotage, and playing the manifest destiny card over and again is just plain wrong.

Too many live life under the volcano, waiting for the eruption. Too many settle for crumbs, and live in the margins.

Even imagination has gone down for the count. Our third eye is so badly bruised and beaten, blackened, that we forget that there just may be life after capitalism.

- to M. Albert, L. Sargent, T. Wetzel

GEORGE TIRADO has been called the Poet Laureate of the Mission District and poetic ambassador from Aztlan - a real life story of race, real estate, and addiction underneath the glitz of gentrification. Tirado toured with the Lollapalooza Spoken Word stage and has shared the stage with many writers, including Lydia Lunch and Jack Hirschman.

BABIES AND BULLETS

Children don't seem to smile as much as they used to. Their emotions are frozen like gunshots in time. Gunshots don't even faze their young eyes. Eyes that used to twinkle with the promise of a penny or a birthday or Christmas now house the shadow of death. It's like if you look deep enough and you are allowed to enter, you will see your death, their death, my death.

Bang! Bang! Bang!
It's all over, but the screaming remains.

Dumpster housing drips with lost American dreams and I'm seeing young brown kids beaten down by ignorant laws which keep their beings drowning in concrete rivers of sadness and sorrow.

Bang! Bang! Bang!
It's all over but the death stare remains.

Only to see what's left of this world in one last gasp: bloody clothes, crying mother, uninterested onlookers, and Jesus Christ this story don't even have a good ending, don't even make the front page.

Bang! Bang! Bang!
It's all over but the memory remains.

Young kids mimic cool homeboy TV heroes and fight to see who can be the tuff guy, because the tuff guy don't feel pain, because the tuff guy don't cry. If this tuff guy is cool enough he might get a gun, and a pocket full of dope, a lot of money and a pair of Air Jordans if he's lucky.

Bang! Bang! Bang!
It's nothing but a dream, the bad dream remains.

No time to play or be a kid any longer. Because you're no longer here. Keep your eyes closed. Like I said, you are no longer here and keep your mouth closed because now you're a man.

Bang! Bang! Bang!
Don't let them shoot you in the face.

MISIDENTIFICTION

I stand alone and look into their eyes
their faces so angry
No one smiles, hands hidden
and crossed behind their backs
shows me a chest wide open for
confrontation

No one smiles in the city of St. Francis
Not when you are misidentified through
popular stereotypes
And all they really know is you are
dangerous to urban society

ANGELS

Martin Luther King once said, "I have a dream"
so did I you see I dreamed in techno
blood red and cuz 415 blue you see

LAST NIGHT I DREAMED OF ANGELS, ANGELS!
in the early morning tenderloin crack crawl
with split lips and blackened eye and broken

wings hoping that this next hit might
make her fly

LAST NIGHT I DREAMED OF ANGELS, ANGELS!
dirty young man smelling of cheap Cisco wine he
removes his clothing and steps away from his
basket then does a drunk tai chi dance naked
in front of god and all the laughing masses

LAST NIGHT I DREAMED OF ANGELS,ANGELS
a tired old man with yellow stained fingers dirty face
snot on beard, hands me his last twenty without
looking down rounds the corner then he's gone

LAST NIGHT I DREAMED OF ANGELS, ANGELS!
youngsters tagging sagging and flagging great walls
with inscriptions only they can read but put there
unto death

LAST NIGHT I DREAMED OF ANGELS, ANGELS
angels   angels
floating   falling and drifting
angelic prostitutes dresses in torn red silk
prom dresses with beat up faces broken bones
falling
spiraling
floating
they reach for their date which is death
he dresses in a red tuxedo he hands them
a dead red rose wrapped in a red ribbon
tonight they will cry hold him close and never let him go
tonight he will laugh and not let them stumble
floating   dreaming
on celestial dream music

LAST NIGHT I DREAMED OF ANGELS

509 YEARS

I was born into two worlds... one of the earth... my skin browned by the sun, and my heart charged with the power of the sun... and my mind able to contemplate the complexities of the Gods.

We have built the pyramids to the skies and our calendar is 2000 years advanced, and our language was that of poets, in our world we were warriors and kings.

But I was born here in this world, Amerikkka, born at the bottom of the ladder with a big black boot of oppression across my neck and more bullet holes in my back then I care to count. But I still wake up everyday reading "WELCOME TO A CLEANER AND WHITER MISSION DISTRICT."

509 years
509 years
509 years

So you can label me and my brothers gangsters, thugs and thieves. So they can fill their pockets with your American government's dope and sell it to some white twenty-year-olds so they to can know what it's like to live on the streets and become animals.

509 years
509 years
509 years

And they told me the invasion was over... Hell no, it ain't over now it's called progress, and look out another 6 million dollar man can come in and steal our land, our homes so he can feel hip with his fast food sushi, and six dollar cups of coffee, his work loft spaces, and the rest of his multi-death corporations...

509 years
509 years
509 years

And with all this comes more racist cops so you and him, his boyfriend and her girlfriend can feel safe from who? Me or them!

I'm bleeding, and I'm dying... beaten like a dog and left in the gutter dying...

HEY MAN YOU DON'T KNOW ME, AND YOU CAN'T BEGIN TO UNDERSTAND MY WORLD

509 years
509 years
509 years

So now I'll tell you who I am
Yo soy Jose Montoya
Yo soy Joquin Murieta
Yo soy Pancho Villa
Yo soy Zapata
Yo soy Ché
Yo soy Fidel Castro
Yo soy Subcommandante Marcos
Yo soy Zapatista Movement

509 years
509 years
509 years

And can't you see the revolution is here, it's not only for land or money... But housing, health care, and to not be treated like an animal

509 years
509 years
509 years

And all I want back is my language and with it I'll say fuck all those propositions like 187 or 21 and the rest

509 years
509 years
509 years

And someone give us back Aztlan

509 years
509 years
509 years

Remember "We didn't cross your borders, they crossed us..."

SILENT FRIEND

Silent, empty body lies in crucifixion position
arms outstretched eyes cold lovingly point up and distant

Unapproachable before but now you are open to all
No access to you is denied, death has come my friend

And with your permission has taken your essence, your life's blood
And left no cheap letter to downplay the act

No rhyme or reason
No excuse to go on fighting

You just let go my dear friend with such ease
Was his personality frightening

Like the thought of you being left alone to endure this
Frozen to death in ice cubes of emotions

Were his eyes soft and kind?
Did he hug you? or touch you?

Did he wipe the sweat from your forehead?
Such a private moment to be shared by someone
who did not even know you

WAR

I'm afraid to close my eyes
Because I'm afraid I won't wake up.

I'm afraid to walk through my city
For fear of tumbling bricks from government buildings.

I'm afraid of this misplaced nationalism which will turn to hatred.

I'm afraid of opening my mouth for
fear of condemning myself in society court
of blindness and intolerance.

I'm afraid my own mother believes
I'm as evil as this unseen enemy is
because any freedom is now in question.

I'm afraid America the Beautiful will
become unholy, and the wonderful sounds of
ageless Muslim singers prayers in ageless mosques
of eternity will never be heard
prayers will go unanswered and
towns and empty streets will not
have a song for God's own ears
And how can you trust a God that don't dance?

And I'm afraid our angry eyes will
see nothing but our own pain.

2ND CLASS TRAIN IN MEXICO

Unsettling whistlestop condemned train moves
and shakes to unimportant destinations.

Baby girl dressed in dirty diapers dances
and slides down floors covered in beer, piss, and water.

With the persistence of a Sunday morning evangelist,
a Mexican shrimp salesman pushes fresh shrimp in the middle of the desert.

Looks from faces chiseled from what we would have called death,
they call life
which at one time produced Aztec gods and Toltec goddesses.

Now hands 2000 pesos to a corrupt conductor
who screams at a man
while he pushes his fist deep into his pocket.

Old dried up woman what we would have called death
at one time they call
saintly, holy, motherly barking table grapes to the masses.

Did César die in vain?

Young Mexican hip-cats drink gallons of Tecate beer, smoke
miles of cheap Mexican cigarettes, and play games of dominoes.

Slapping down spotted bones to assert power with
great tales of never-ending panochas.
I've never been in a culture so lost between two worlds.

But it's good to know that Coca-Cola has a strong foothold here.

FROM MY HEART REVOLUTION

Last night I dreamed I was an Aztecan warrior proud,
standing high atop a pyramid my long black hair blowing in
the wind. Now I'm here in the barrio. I am here alone watching
as young soldiers are rounded up nightly: hands behind head,
legs crossed in the back. Their faces violently pushed into
murals of the Virgin Mary or her son. I watch as flashing lights
make shadow imagery on the faces of uninterested onlookers—
red for the north and blue for the south.

My ears are filled with the dull beat of sad hearts and crying
loose talk I-told-you-sos in both English and Spanish. The

sad songs from the passing mariachis and the same tired old symphonies I hate, made from the sirens of the chotas cruisers.

I am lost and confused. My culture is dying. I see it everywhere, like that dead mother's son whose only place is a dirty sidewalk, that with his last breath and last moment the only thing he takes in is a restaurant which tells us to run for the border and this is what killed him to start with.

Remember we did not all cross the border before it killed us.

All my heroes are gone fighting revolutions, this time they might win. Juan Murrieta's head is in a jar of alcohol. The brown buffalo is dead in a cornfield with a spike hanging out of his arm. Ché is killed by the same people who one day may kill us all, and Mumia pounds his head on a concrete wall hoping someone will understand.

I put down the pipe. I put down the needle. I pick up a pen, and now I see Aztlan as it is meant to be seen: infinite, forever.

IN MEMORY OF MY GRANDMA

I'm sitting here in the city of San Francisco. It's late but not late enough that the clouds have not claimed the sun turning the sky black.

But now I'm thinking of you, Grandma, and I'm not thinking of the pain that you have lived through, or the pain of the cancer, but of the gift you and Ma gave me. I'm thinking of your wrinkled hands molded from the earth, the same earth that colored your skin brown, that made our culture flourish for thousands of years. Of your smile charged from the sun.

But now I'm thinking about the little things, like the smells of beans and rice, a humbling meal, soul food coated with spices from the old world. And I think about how me and Mark would steal fresh tortillas from the grill and put them under our shirts turning our young bellies red. And we would laugh.

Or how you would pronounce my name we would laugh and spend hours walking through flea markets, feet tired through Phoenix days. Then drink glass after glass of o.j. made from the oranges growing outside.

But now you've gone. You have joined the other ancestors on that journey back to Aztlan, back to the top of the pyramid, to the heart of the sun, to the middle of forever, and when you get there, Grandma, and you see my dad tell him I miss him. Rest in Peace.

TAMAYO, PAINTER OF LA RAZA

Tamayo, painter of La Raza, I hide behind every stroke of your brush—through violence, through love. Through your eyes, I've searched out my culture. People move to the sounds of the church bells. They wear black veils and carry flowers to the graves of our ancestors and pray to the dead. Colors sustain life in a culture of desolation and barren realization, whitewashed to hide poverty.

La Raza's muddy hands carefully spin pottery, and faces of the potter are in constant contemplation. Eyes dark like the night that holds the secret hidden by you, by time, through life and death which soon become the same, no difference. Play hide and go seek behind your brushstroke, Tamayo, through your eyes I have seen Mexico. Through your strokes, we felt that which has been hidden forever because of words, culture, and because of hatred.

Boy with ripped shirt plays a beat on an ageless drum into the future. Is there a place for him there? Is there a place for me here? Or do skulls sitting at the base of a Toltec God hold the only promise for me?

Tamayo, behind your strokes do you laugh at time, God, or just people? Just that simple? Or do you understand yourself? I've lost myself behind your walls, dragged myself through life only to stand here in frustration. In a room full of stars, the darkness won't seem so painful after all.

POESIA

This guy once asked me "Why don't you write like Pablo Neruda?"

I laughed as I found my favorite spot on 16th and Mission. It was cold, the morning sun had not found its way out yet, and the wind froze me to my being.

You know, I contemplated why I don't write like Pablo Neruda as I pushed my fist deep into the pockets of my black trench coat and waited for the bus. It was at this minute my senses came to life. I inhaled deep the smells of stagnant water mixed with false courage, exhaust fumes, and early morning Joneses, along with the endless shuffling of street hustlers running between the dealers and junkies wishing for a free wake up.

There is nothing more promising then the twinkle in the eye of an early morning score when you know everything is good. The two street preachers on both sides of the street scream—one in Spanish, the other English—to this ugly world, hoping to save one soul. Even the prostitutes' names are not pretty and their game is just as old.

In the corner of my eye I see Satan lurking in the shadows, he's dressed in his favorite hoodie. He talks to his girls on his cell phone; he calls them bitches and hoes, then he waits. And all I want to see is Jesus Christ himself come down and show mercy on these souls and give them all an immaculate fix like ten million golden speedballs exploding in their souls, leaving them to sidewalk surf between their unforgettable high and reality.

Why don't I write like Pablo Neruda?

A MARCH

sweat drips from my forehead to ground
my heart pumps faster and faster,
feet march in perfect order,
amongst the chaos,
arms raised, fist clenched,
punching the sky,

almost saying to an indifferent god,
"stop me if you can."
i hold the hand of a girl from chiapas
she is dressed all in black
everything covered except her eyes,
her eyes tell me all I need to know
in her eyes I see the pain of war,
in her eyes I see the loss of brothers and sisters,
in her eyes I see the anger of colonialism
it is with this anger I dream I dream of a huge fuse
that would be lit with this rage
and it will explode under nike town,
freeing all ten-year-old sweatshop workers
from their chains bound to mike jordan
so they now can play like mike
it would explode under starbucks
ending this coffee empire
so the jungles in south america
can be replanted
to the way they were,
and indigenous farmers can sell
their own coffee
and feed their own people
it would explode under cartier
freeing the poor miners in south africa
it would explode under every prison here in califas
freeing all political prisoners of aztlan
it would explode under the metreon
shaking up hollywood
it would explode under everyone involved in
gentrification anywhere who purposely
kicked people out of their homes so they could take
over, leaving families homeless
but I blink my eyes and I'm back, her hands are rough,
like my mother's,
her voice is loud like the screams of the thousand
silenced people
she is hard like a soldier,
she is proud
she is a mother giving birth to a new revolution

she is my comrade and today we march together hand in hand
across the street an old cuban man holds up a poster
of Ché with his tired right hand and his left one
makes a fist in the air smiling as he screams
"power to the people"

THE VOYEURS

There is no such thing as a good day or a bad day.... He wrote in his dirty notebook, shaking to put the words down. Beads of sweat fell random from his forehead through canyons carved deep into his skin and dripped onto paper. It don't mean if it's cold or wet, or hot, the days are all the same. It depends on how fast they make you move. King wrote the last of his thoughts down on the notepad and sat back in his chair looking out the window; the reflection from the clock flashed over and over almost haunting him: 3 a.m. "It's still too fucking early," he whispered.

Taking another long drag from his smoke and filling his lungs, he shifted his weight in the chair; not only because his leg was asleep (which was the only part of him that would sleep today), but thanks to the woman who rented the room across the air shaft. She was concentration camp skinny, a crackhead who lived on nothing but Jack-in-the-Box hamburgers, Dr. Peppers, and large amounts of crack cocaine. She never seemed to change her clothes either. She wore an ugly torn nightgown, blue he thought, with enough holes that nothing was ever really covered. King watched from the window as he always did. For him it was better than TV. He never could seem to keep a television anyways. This was real.

She knew he watched, and he knew she let him watch. That's what made this so perfect. After watching her run through her many tricks, blowing and fucking slobs from the building, scoring for her dope, and then watching her get burned for her last $20 bill and running manic around her room, King would laugh as he watched her naked body on all fours like a dog crying just to find a piece. She would be mumbling something he could never make out. To him it sounded like speaking in tongues, like he had seen in some old film footage about snake worshipers, and poison drinkers. To King she was no longer female, her skinny body and busted up face, her sagging, shriveled breasts, and the flesh which hung from her bones made her look surreal instead.

Another smoke and a glance at that flashing clock: 3:20 and all was well, he thought. He reached over and turned on the radio, found some classic rock station, put his feet up and closed his eyes. Tonight even dreams of a bogeyman would be better than no dreams at all.

Just as the sun first peaked its head over the red brick building, King was up sorting out and trying to collect his wits. Even before his spirit was up, his body was almost out the door. The only thing he really had to do was throw on his dirty old black trenchcoat, and fill his mouth with six balloons of fake dope he picked up over the years. And put the 30 bucks he'd been saving into his pants pocket and headed out into the world.

It was a regular San Francisco Mission District morning. Cold, not enough to freeze you but just enough to piss you off, and it was raining, not drops but that mist that sticks to your body and leaves that mildew smell on everything once it warms up.

King headed towards the spot around the corner, averting his eyes down so not to look at anyone in case he ran into someone that he had burned. In his mind, this gave him just enough invisibility to stay one step ahead of the collectors, and one step ahead of someone who was going to kick his tired old ass. But he moved slow. To him this was not new, but a chore he'd been doing for years. He knew the game, nodded to whores who passed by calling him Big Daddy, acknowledged the old junkies who would whisper in that tired old junkie way, "What's up, King? Are ya holdin', brother?"

"No, but Cuba's around." Little was said, just a nod, when from the Burger King, King saw his man. An old Cuban the longtime junkies could count on for a full count on short money. Just standing and watching the early morning traffic of young dealers who use and abuse their own customers for a laugh. King walked up, looked Cuba in the eyes and whispered, "Hey, Cuba, can you do five for thirty?"

GEORGE

Lighting a smoke, King took a deep drag, and before he knew it, Cuba had said, "Si." Handing over the money, King keep an eye out for the law. This was the time when you feel most venerable. Cuba reached into his pants like he was scratching his nuts and removed five red balloons and handed them to him. King smiled, "Thanks, homes." He stuffed his fist deep into his coat pockets.

Just as quick as he scored his dope, King was heading back until he looked up and saw a punk rocker kid. You could not have missed him: tired, frayed spiked hair faded from years of bad dye jobs, ripped up blue jeans and this old faded black leather jacket. "Chiva? Chiva?" he whispered as he passed folks in front of the Chinese restaurant.

King heard him, spit the balloons out into his hand, and said, "Yeah," as he passed the kid. "I got six." Kid shot back, "I got forty, come on old man, do me right." King slipped the balloons into the hand of the kid and watched as the kid headed toward the BART station. King laughed to himself as he disappeared into the bathroom long enough to not only hide but count his money.

"Assholes born everyday. Old man? What the fuck was that?" Freedom today. He had enough to get high on later and a few extra bucks to slip into the Roxy for a film. It was a good day.

"Nothing like beating a mark before breakfast," King joked. Today was the best of all possibilities, nothing like holding enough dope and money so your mind wouldn't overwork itself.

King laughed. Reaching his room, it all became a ritual. "Go for the box," he would whisper. Finding it, he would then remove his coat, fill his cup with water, remove his spoon, break the end off the cigarette, make a small ball of cotton. The whole time his breath slowed down, waiting for the rush, placing the dope from the balloons in the spoon. Add water with the new U-120 King—liked the long spike, easier to hit the vein—then fire. His mouth, dry from the anticipation. He swallows the last of his spit, draws up the dope, fills the point to the 80 line and smiles. Probing his arm, he found a spot, sticking the point in, register cheek for blood, perfect hit. He takes a deep breath. "Nothin' like going downtown.

Shit," King whispers. Something's wrong. His body convulses, jerking. He forces his eyes open. He knows what happened. King, played for an OD.

King fought to breathe. "It's so slow," he thought. Half his body had gone numb. He looked out his window, the woman across the alley was watching. She saw him shake and gasp for air. She watched as the spike fell from his arm into darkness. King fought to keep his eyes open—*there ain't no angels singing no white lights*—he watched as the woman began to cry. One tear. She waved. He grasped at the closed window. Sliding from his chair, he watched as she turned and walked off, then darkness.

Outside of the window, a young kid sold his fist rock, tucked the first ten into his pocket. Today, he is king.

RAW KNOWLEDGE is a working-class firebrand proud of her anarchist politics. She has a full-length CD entitled *Nemesis to Silence* and appears on the compilation *Bread and Roses* (Entartete Kunst Records).

AT FIVE O'CLOCK IN THE EVENING

It's 5 o'clock I got the call,
and I'm holding myself
as these tears flow going against my
heart and the voices in my head
that tell me to be strong.
I'm strong
I'm strong
I punch the air wishing it was
the faces of the judge, jury, the fucking
pigs who nabbed you, and the system
that makes us who we are.

And now it's 5:20 and this pain
in my chest is moving slowly to my gut and
I'm thinking about time,
thinkin' about the next few years to come
how being behind bars leaves family,
lovers, and friends locked up there with you
and my tears can't stop flowing.

I wish little brother
that I could have kept my promise
my big hopes and dreams
hit rock bottom, and I'm trying
to save myself, save the future and
I'm trying
I'm trying hard to be strong,
and everyday I talk and smile
at faces who never care to know
our tales of struggle,
who never care to know
our tales of crying

crying out for help
reaching for a hand up only to get a
slap, kick in the face and
handcuffs as option,
It's 5:39 and I see you
facing time,
I want to tear the walls down,
not just for you
but all the innocent guilty of
being born poor, my hands
are clinched tight and I know
I gotta keep it together,
We gotta keep it together
I'm trying
It's 5:40 now and I feel the gavel of the judge crushing
that imposed liberal notion that
we can have what we need if we
believe in god, country and government.
It's bleeding
I'm bleeding
It's 6:00 little brother and
our pain, anger, frustration and love
is fuel, my faith in keeping
up the struggle for liberation
the fight for freedom
the plight to destroy the slave master who
never emancipated any of us,
they haven't given me
any
other choice!

R.I.P. LIL' G

Twisted maimed bodies
casualties of war
wheelchair bound
if not prison or early death

it comes
and goes
the thoughts
to leave it all behind,
but the fight
is all that is left?

Can't go back
don't want to
visit
hated home,
fighting for the
hood I hate

to live in
striving for and end,
the bullet
going to
ending up
flying back
at me

mama prays
pops beats
ALWAYS been the
world's bastard child
told to
"Just say no!"
to
violence,
drugs,
my language,
my heritage.

You think we are much different?

Because this rage
is all you have left behind
our violence almost mirrored
by that same government

that uses its guns and drug money
to kill
in El Salvador, Haiti, Uganda, India,
Vietnam, Bosnia, Ireland, Texas, Ohio,
Philadelphia, New Your, Oakland, Detroit,
LA!

Theirs they say is
justified,
"Seek and Destroy"
A learned tactic
expressed by all those
who obtain power?

Jailed,
maimed,
dead,
casualties
of the war fought
by many
displaced soldiers.

CLASS WAR

*"And if today we fall without compromising
we can be sure of victory tomorrow."- Malatesta*

So here they go again
They same promises spoken
to be broken
to serve those in power,
while we scrub their floors,
take their orders, serving
always selling
our aching bodies,
our neglected children, our lives
to their wars, their science, to
live to see the repeat of another day.

The fight that's always been
the point to our resistance
was never
between skin,
but the profit reaped off from it,
a class war
putting, pitting us all against each other
dog eat dog survival
death
denial, and blind allegiance to a dream
of empires, kings, queens, gods, goddesses.
Who's your daddy, your leader, your god,
your master?

The question spoken by the 20%
who use it to keep the 80% in
"our place"
our lives and those of the people
around the world
move up and down on the Dow Jones
expendable we are
and still slaving to consume the products
we built,
only to have to give it back to us
in bullets, handcuffs, coffins, and disease
hidden underneath the land
they seek to privatize.

The fight that's always been
the point of our resistance
was never
between skin,
but the profit reaped off from it,
a class war,
a so-called case study
that has yet to end the trail of tears of 1838
it's been spreading and repeating
spilling
in the ocean, in the food, buried
in or communities

buried deep, deeper than the truth
behind the lies beaming on TV.
deceit on the tongues of those who
control to corrupt
and these candidates keep talking,
as their debt keeps acquiring
for us the underprivileged to pay
and so the symptoms of capital gain
are lived through by the
manifestations of oppression
in the form of
racism, sexism, depression, addiction
once again overlooked is the burden
of carrying the floor
to the aristocracy

I say the fight that's
always been the point to our resistance
was never between skin
but the profit reaped off of it,
it's a class war!

RUNAWAYS

The intensity in my heart pound so loud that my footsteps
are lighter. I took all I could; I carry it on my back fiercely,
but strapped upon me nonetheless. I've been running, running
for what seems to be years. Each step, each tread, brings me
closer and farther away from what I left behind. I run. I can
see their faces. Mother, her face weary, arms stretched out
wanting to bring me to her heart; but the arms pulling me
away from her are stronger.

I sleep, resisting my head under my hands. I have dreams.
Dreams of pleasantries that turn bleak as all returns to
nightmares, and light the fire to keep me running against. "Stay
away from the roads, follow the river, keep your eye on the
Northern Star," I remember my father telling me at a time I
can't help but try to forget. I put his words to the test as the

hounds are on my trail, seething teeth sharp to cut me down, I run. "Don't look back," I hear in my head, so I don't but at times my lips remember the fondness of that first kiss, the warmth of the embrace, the sweat, of that night in the sweat that runs from my brow now. Does she think of me? He keeps me running. I run.

I grow weary, I grow, and I grow accustomed to the night. She moves me forward, so forward I go, relinquishing all that said, "I'll be there," all that said, "I'm sorry," all that hated and begged me to stay. Each step says hello, I run.

I mend my wounds; I cover up the scars. None dare to see the imbedded puncture wounds, this land smells of blood, so I must layer the bandages to keep the sharks from tasting and wanting to swallow me whole. I run. You run faster.

O brother, I won't forget you. Courageously, you take the straps across your back. I see your scars, too! I want to scoop you up into my arms but I know all about the arms that pull you away from me. I'll treasure you. "Stay strong." Strong are my legs, I run.

I'm a runaway slave, shackles of lies around my wrist. Injustice binding my legs. I carry hope in my heart. I run. I carry the past in my head. I run. I carry my anger in my gut. I run. I run away from, I run into. I run with future's destiny in front of me. I run, I run, I run, I'm running. Follow the North Star and I'll meet you there too! We are all runaways.

FASHION STARVATION

The government says
there aren't enough
jobs,
money,
resources,
to help the poor and suffering people of the world.

MEANWHILE...

Children are crying.
The media talks
of billion dollar corporate money laundering schemes
that has left the Dow Jones at another low from yesterday

MEANWHILE...

The cries have turned into whimpers.

Bill Clinton talks of his "leadership" and
thousands were given from Hollywood to a perpetrator
of genocide not just in Columbia, Kosovo, Somalia
and in between the span of the world but in
America as well.

MEANWHILE...

The whimpers of the children
have become labored as nausea continues
and the smell of acetone makes starvation smell fruity.
Bush keeps talking about
"terrorism."
"cowardly acts,"
and
"infinite justice,"
as his strategies on decreasing violence
has left blood on everyone's hands.

MEANWHILE...

Nature is kinder in death
than the power hungry politicians
as a lethargic sleep
eases the pain of slow death.

The poor continue to starve
to save replicated 1980 S&L bailouts

MEANWHILE...

Starvation attacks the kidney,
liver,
brain,
an infection and disease consume the body.

The well-off continue to plunder
destroy and terrorize for profits
as the toxic sludge in impoverished communities
continues to contaminate

You sit there a slave to fashion
sigh
and say to me
"I don't want to spend my life
fighting for a change that may never happen."

MEANWHILE...

Invalidism if not death
is creeping up on another life
and as another victim dies from starvation
in exchange for your "sense of style"
I hope you wanting to hasten the death of your own life
is worth murdering others.

MURDER ON THE MIND

Sometimes you take
all you can stand.
Some say not to be angry
but freedom rests outside the barbed wire
worse than being in your homeland?
Six years later and asylum still hasn't come...
the rage turns to murder on the mind.

You fight for justice, they give you handcuffs.
You want life, they trade yours for their greed.
Taking your value for granted
Their lives before your truth.

You took all that you could
Their life or yours turns to murder on the mind.

Time has a way of rotting you out,
leaving only a testimony of nightmares and lies.
Behind every plastic smile—a lie,
behind every new report—a lie
behind every authority—a lie.

And then like the creeping fog
you get murder on the mind.

PACIFY TO JUSTIFY

It goes
the lies exposed
underneath
the truth is much harder to believe.

Scenarios, scenes of crimes set up
they're good and it's been done
so many times
easy we are to fool
we their tools
to pacify
to justify
the blood on their hands
as we continue to put our heads in the sand.

It goes, the lies exposed
underneath
the truth is much harder to believe.

The betrayal of democracy
go ahead, read the entrails
you still won't see
that behind every government
is the slaughter of innocence
to pacify

to justify

And it goes
the lies exposed
underneath
the truth is much harder to believe.

Greed
Oppression
Destruction
pray to your appeasing government
as it serves up your
life as a burnt offering
to the annihilation of life.

BROTHER'S KEEPERS

I AM MY BROTHER'S KEEPER
Who better a keeper than a creature
who is the keeper to many sons and daughters
I AM MY BROTHER'S KEEPER
I keep my brother from falling
prey to stupid lies on MTV
I keep my brother smart,
I keep my brother thinking,
I keep my brother,
My brother keeps me.

My brother will cut his own throat
to give me my voice,
I keep my brother,
who keeps my image my womanly ways
respected as the keeper of life,
I keep him.
He keeps me.
No one else
will keep my brother
All of them on death row, my

brother's dying in this
the only hell,
My brothers who live hard, fast lives,
My brothers misrepresented
My brothers
ALL

I am your keeper.

NATIONAL SECURITY

It's a matter of national security,
that you've been lied to, that you've been
cut out of all negotiations for the advancement of your life.
It's a matter of national security,
that you keep swallowing the white lie
in the form of Prozac and Xanax,
keep well and secure in this state of democracy,
brought to you by...
slick business people bent on turning us all into
robots of mindless consumption.

Step up to the counter boys and girls,
who's next in line to be served?
Outside of some pollution would you like
some manufactured chemicals with that slab of
genetically altered animal flesh?
Wash it down with a bottle of national pride,
be sure to wipe to corners of your mouth with some
fanatical religion
because...

It's a matter of national security
that you keep ignorant in this country of complacency.
It's a matter of national security
that you believe you are safe, until
they come for you,
because your apathy is imperative to national security

REFUSE AND RESIST

Globalization
is Imperialism's new name
as the same rhetoric of "let democracy prevail"
of 1964
is its battle cry
to justify
the commencement of war,
today,
on anyone who does not OBEY...
the giant
the new OLD World order of
the conquest of 1492
that keep repeating its
arrival on foreign shores, by sending shrapnel
through the sky
and another life dies for another war,
another war,
another newscast that won't report
on another holocaust kept blind from view
that starves another Iraqi child, as
another Haitian body washed ashore
capitalism expands its war, as another
stillborn birth happens in Hamilton, Ohio,
another kid kills himself on Turtle Mountain,
as another piece of legislation is conspired to
bring justice to another victim of the police state,
that Christian Parenti says "doesn't exist yet,"
as another cop fires a bullet
taking a life that was meant to live, that capitalism tainted
for corporate profit like the constitution
I wipe my ass with
and if we keep giving the system validation through
elected revolutionaries it will be
another four years where we
dig our own graves for another
war for profit the rich say
is the end to all our suffering...
To live freely is to RESIST!

THE DEFIANT ONES

"Can you fly?" they asked him.
They joked that he screamed like a "fucking woman..."
Teeth glistening, they said, "Are you man enough?"

Seconds ripped through his mind. He remembered what brought him here. The look on his father's face as he buried him practically with his bare hands. He remembered his mother's eyes. He had her eyes, now blurred from the blood streaming down from the wound on his forehead. They tortured him until he had no feeling in his legs. His body was still shaking from the strategically placed electro-clamps on his skin, but he would not give in. The one memory played over and over again in his mind. The one that gave birth to the revolutionary. The soldiers, the guns, the villagers, bulldozed homes, forced evictions, starvation, dead bodies; piled almost to the sky, this was the fate of many, and he knew it. Those dictators of destruction, those CEOs, sealed and delivered with a vengeance an unbearable despair that could only be met, fought, and won through resistance.

"Can you fly?" they asked of him.
Grabbing him, gripping him outside the helicopter...
The teeth of the soldier shined in the light of the sun
assuming fear and intimidation would yield information...

A calmness spread over his bruised face.
He yelled with what little strength he had left.
A defiant "Yes!"

The soldier smiled and
simply
just let
go.

QUEST FOR LIFE

I'm tired of being ready to die. I'm tired of that stupid phrase being replayed, replayed, and replayed, as if it makes you hard. How about being ready to live? I want to live. My quest in achieving this sentiment makes me more prepared to obtain it. Being ready to live, living means that you are already a bad ass, because you will defend the rights of yourself and others without the greed that makes living this life so fucking hard. I'm ready to live for myself. I'm ready to live for the many that died, the many who were murdered. The children Afghanistan who have died before their fifth birthday due to starvation, for the bottle children in Mexico, for the homeless children in Brazil, for the children who died in the Ludlow Massacre of 1914, for the young people who died in the 1976 Soweto student protest, and those who continue to die. I'm going to live.

Through my living I will fight for the women who have given their lives to better the world, women like Fannie Sellins murdered by deputies in Pennsylvania 1919 while trying to keep children out of danger during a strike against the Allegheny Coal and Coke Company, rebels like Elizabeth Flynn. Who killed Judi Bari? I want those responsible for her cancer held accountable. I'm gonna live for the men who gave their lives to fight wars for greedy businessmen. I'm gonna live because George Engel, before being executed on November 11th, 1887 in court during his sentencing said, "...every thoughtful person must combat a system which makes it possible for the individual to rake and hoard millions in a few years while on the other side thousands become tramps and beggars."

My life is dedicated to the memory of Albert Nun Washington and Fred Hampton. I'm fighting for Carlo Giuliani murdered in Genoa 2001. I'm living for the 30,000 kidnapped and murdered Argentinian women, men, and children who died in the Dirty War of 1970 at the hands of a corrupt government sponsored by the CIA. The hundreds of Ethiopian citizens who have and continue to disappear in that country since the US/CIA-sponsored elections. I'm going to live for the three Zimbabwean political prisoners, Phillip Conjwayo,

Mike Smith, and Kevin Wood who have been incarcerated since 1988 from the South African apartheid era.

I will live for the living in exile and those locked up in this country and abroad for opposing immoral corporate government legislation: Assata Shakur, Herman Bell, Cuban political prisoner Manuel Villa Espinosa, Jihad Abdul Mummit, Marilyn Buck, Irish political prisoner in Belfast Davy Adams, Tom Manning, Yu Kikimura, Richard Williams, Sylvia Baraldini,, Irish political prisoner in Derry Martina Anderson, Bill Dunne, Puerto Rican Nationalist Alberto Rodriguez, ALF member Rod Coronado, Carmen Sims Africa, Marshall Edward, Larry Gidding, Jaan Karl Laaman, Lori Berenson, the 5000 Peruvians in prison since the 1992 coup and numerous other men women and children who are in prison simply because they too made the decision to be ready to live.

I put forth a challenge to everyone listening. I challenge you to live, to challenge a system that perpetuates racism, sexism, terrorism, greed, and countless other ill wills off the backs and dead bodies of the poor and working class women, men and children. Maybe if you take upon this challenge to live it will become contagious enough to spread to the projects of Hunter's Point, the streets of Glasgow, the hills of Appalachia, the hills of Chiapas, the whorehouses in Singapore, the diamond mines in South Africa, the allies in Calcutta, and just maybe through the long process of self-determination to do more than just fucking survive all of us as one collective body can stand as a solid wall in solidarity with the Zapatistas, the COBAS in Italy, the South African Student Organization, the Anarchist Black Cross, the many women, men, prisoners of war, and political prisoners, and once and for all give a big FUCK YOU to the prisoners of the Earth, the greedy multimillionaires, the imperialistic government, the liberal hippie democratic left, and dictators who continue to rape everyone of us of our humanity, who continue to bully us into slave wage jobs and poverty. Maybe when we make our lives more valuable all of the impending bullshit put forth by these bastards will stop and all of us will be free, free to live!

LEROY MOORE is the founder of the Disability Advocates for Minorities organization. He lectures frequently on disability rights and issues facing working class people of color. His columns appear in the Bayview newspaper and *Poor* magazine. His work has been recognized by KQED Public Television and the San Francisco Board of Supervisors.

A DIFFERENT TYPE OF HONEYMOON

Poverty & Disability were forced to get married
no honeymoon
survived slavery, eugenics & Reagan
to give birth to 80% of the disabled population
worldwide & in war-torn countries
while disabled elite live in their highrises

Crack babies bouncing off walls
elders evicted from their homes
Vietnam Vets can't sleep battling on the streets
and what?! Superman wants more money so he can walk!
while Black disabled men are becoming instinct

Men in white suits
Are they doctors, scientists or the KKK?
Tuskegee experiment broke the trust
Sickle Cell, HIV, Cancer & Diabetes
all alone bleeding in the emergency room
and what?! Bush wants bodies for his war!

Chewing on gums
shit even the toothfairy don't
want my rotten teeth
growing old with a physical disability
running after my youth
falling down constantly
wheelchair in the near future
Medical won't pay for a sports chair
sitting in this old hospital chair

Poverty & Disability
at the altar
priest tries holy water but
can't heal it
so our lives become a sin
scratching & clawing
up the capitalist ladder
only to break down
by isms in man's society

Causing mental illness
no treatment or forced treatment
minds on wings of birds flying south
leaving behind scarecrows with no souls
and there's no Dorothy, Oz or a yellow brick road
only the Po Po
concrete that leads to
Chowchilla's skilled nursing home

Poverty & Disability
went to the courts for a divorce
but got time in the pen
while serving they realized
if there is no struggle
there's no progress
so today they aren't afraid to speak
putting everyone on the hot seat
coming together in unity
writing their own vowels
building a community
the struggle is the honeymoon and
the honeymoon is the struggle.

EAT MY DISABILITY!

Open up wide
No salt, no pepper
No seasoning

Knife & Fork
No spoon, no napkin
No drink to wash it down

Eat my disability!

Cut it slice it
In small pieces
Now chew it

Serve it up rare
Like my poetry
With red sauce, my blood
Mixing with your salvia

We are becoming one

A delicate dish
Licking your lips
Surprise, you might like it

Are you ready for seconds!

FIGHTING, TEACHING AND HEALING

America preaches integration but practices segregation
George Washington had a plantation
He left us in a fucked up situation
California is still reacting to Pete Wilson

35 years living under oppression
No wonder there is war in this nation
Poets need to get out our frustration
Give us a mike no more waiting

Black and disabled
Teacher and warrior
Poet and activist
Fighting and teaching in this revolution

War is 24/7
I'm strapped with my AK47
I'll fight until I wake up in heaven
Beat down by race and disability discrimination

War is a bitch
Burying my sisters and brothers in a ditch
While dot-coms were getting rich
Can you understand my reaction?

Give me the stage
This war will make you think
Delivering a healing message to the masses
No more bullshit we're taking action

Revenge is sweet
Poets, it's time to speak
Our art will make you weak
Only love no competition

Stiff in a coffin
But Leroy is laughing
Cause this war has no ending
Only the dead hold the solution

OH MY BROTHER, WHAT HAPPENED TO YOU?

Get down and
Get off
I wonder
Are you my brother?

Get down off that ladder
Get off my neck
My brother you are a wreck
What happened, we used to live together

Related to one another
Racism and capitalism

Now we are killing each other
Somehow you lost your color

Ivory walls
Corporate office halls
Cell phone calls
You have climbed and now you've a long way to fall

Look at you
In your three-piece suit
You think you're so cool
But you're goddamn fool

In your BMW
Pulled over on a DWB
Cops don't care if you've a Ph.D.
Just another nigger they see

Oh my brother
You're out there
Found yourself homeless
No community and no family

Sold your soul
Your mind has been whitewashed
Can't realize
You've been hypnotized

Oh my brother
You got it bad
Sleeping in the master's bed
Why don't you just put a gun to your head?

You are playing with a live wire
Sooner or later your life will go up in fire
One day soon it'll be your turn
Oh my brother you'll get burned

Get down off your pedestal
Get off of my back

MOORE

Come back home
Oh my brother, what happened to you?

SO WHAT'S UP??

You want me
I want you
So what's up?

I got the knowledge
You have a position
So what's up?

You are a millionaire
I am on welfare
So what's up?

I got a wallet
You got a gun
So what's up?

You have a publishing company
I got a book
So what's up?

I am homeless
You are a landlord
So what's up?

We can go on and on
But at night we can't sleep
Cause we both know what's up

THE ARTIST/ACTIVIST

I'm a poet with an activist tongue
I'm an activist with a pen
Words marching in protest across the page

My demands are clear
No need to read between the lines
Black and White fuck the Gray area

I'm an activist with a bullhorn
Shouting "No justice, No peace!"
Slamming revolutionary poetry on open mike night

Nigger with disability
In front of City Hall
Bringing the streets inside Ivory Walls

Words causing a reaction
That leads to action
Pen to paper signing legislation

Politics n poetry
We know who is not down
We've been around before Willie and Jerry Brown

The activist is active
At the ballot and in the community
Gil Scott said The Revolution will Not Be Televised

So turn off the T.V.
And join me
On the streets

Because I'm the Artist/Activist
Spoken word with
The sounds of marching feet

Wondering why I'm alone

The Last Poets said it in the '70s
Now it's the twenty-first century
Still Niggers are scared of revolution

I'm a poet politician

No party for me
I'm not independent
Cause I'm fighting with my brothers and sisters

Cracking the capitalist system
Ending racism, sexism
And all other isms

Like Jesus I'm homeless
Moses was my brother
I'm a teacher and my students are of all colors

My words were censored
But Helen Keller taught
Me American Sign Language

The mainstream can't silence me
Shut down one path
I'll make another

My art is public
I need people
Nothing is private

I live with many

You can call me a hippie
Can't be secluded like a yuppie
That would driving me fucking crazy

The Artist/Activist's life is lonely
Everything I do is
Outside the norms of society

A brother from a different planet

Taking over planet earth
There is no lifeform down here
So beam me up, Scotty

But I can't leave my people in shackles
So watch out
The Artist/Activist is coming to your town

Join the arts & politics campaign
Speaking truth through oral history
That can't be found in dusty books

The Artist/Activist
Wants you, your mother
Grandparents, the spirits of your ancestors
And your firstborn

Creating an army
Who will love and protect our community
Calling out everyone

The elderly, the disabled, the youth
Gays and lesbians
Women and men
All have a job to do

Mix the paints
DJs on the turntables
Poets on the mike
Intellectuals writing speeches

Walking to the capital
We are the people
Taking our rightful seats in the US Congress

Politics could be colorful
If we used everybody's talents
Bill Clinton on the saxophone
But his peers could not feel the rhythm

We need more Artists/Activists
In the White House
But we always end up doing time in the big house

God we are strong
Mumia Abu Jamal tearing down prison walls
Political prisoners speaking to us all

Paul Robeson's words and music lives on
The youth are communicating and fighting through spoken word
The melting pot is on the stove and it's ready to explode

Ha, ha, ha—just can't get enough of the Artist/Activist

THE BLACK RACE, A SKIT

The Black Race is a promotional commercial for a yearly
event in the Black Community.

Characters :   The Host
                 Tom and Dick
                 The Referee
Place: Washington, DC (i.e., The Chocolate City)

Narrated by Leroy Moore

Tom: Hello Dick! It's about that time of year again.

Dick: Yes it is, Tom, and we're expecting more people than
last year. Let's go to the video of last year's BLACK RACE.

VIDEO: Yes, we are here today in Washington, DC, what
those people call the "Chocolate City."

Tom: I can see why, Dick. All I see are niggers, oops, I mean
Black people, for miles.

Dick: The Black Race happens every year all over the
country. For twenty-eight days the whole country can see,
hear read and buy Black American history, culture, art and
literature.

Tom: I love hosting this race, Dick! Seeing and promoting capitalism and exploitation of Black Americans.

Dick : But isn't that America?

Tom: Oh yes it is, Dick. But today the race is more diverse! I mean you've got Black women, gays and lesbians, and Black disabled people putting in their two cents.

Dick : Tom, I hope they have more than two cents. You got to have money for this race.

Tom: But isn't it amazing how those people come out every year to exploit themselves on our behalf and to fit their culture and history into the shortest month of the year! It is just amazing!

Dick : We're about to begin the race. Let's go down to the starting line.

The Referee: Listen up! Listen up! Welcome to the 1999 Black Race. Here are the rules:

1) Like every year, the Black Race is only for twenty-eight days. After the 28th, we don't want to see or hear from you until next year!
2) This race is about how much you can give to the market and that means nothing is free. Sell, charge, just get that money!
3) The Race must be diverse.
4) Always remember rules number one and two.
ON YOUR MARK GET SET GO!!

Dick: Look at them run.

Tom: It's going to be an exciting but short month. Well, we're your hosts, Dick and Tom.

Dick: You've got twenty-eight days to watch The Black Race.

Tom: Yeah, don't miss it cause there will not be any reruns.

Tom and Dick: This is Tom and Dick in The Chocolate City, Washington, DC. We'd like to thank our official sponsors of the Black Race, Kentucky Fried Chicken and Nike.

END OF VIDEO, BACK TO TOM AND DICK

Tom and Dick: Well, that was a clip from last year's Black Race. Join us in Atlanta, Georgia for the first Black Race of 2000.

WHAT CAN I DO?

I cry, pry and lay down to think
I'm frustrated, fed up and angry
Lately my positive attitude and all that I do
Is in the trash with the kitchen sink

My poems & articles are not enough
Being Black and disabled is rough
I'm wound up tight
Watch out I might go off

Death all around
Blood up to my knees
Screams in my dreams
The future looks bleak

What can I do?
No role models
No path to follow
Mom is gone and I'm lost in this battle
Walking on thin ice
That's my life
I need a retreat
So I can relax and sleep

Organize and advocate
Caught between reality and Uncle Sam's red tape
Can't help my brothers and sisters
Cause I'm buried under government papers

What can I do?
All avenues lead to a dead end
Margaret L. Mitchell, Kelvin Robinson and James Byrd
All dead, will this brutality ever end?

Marcus Hogg hog-tied
Noose around his neck
Society needs to realize
Disabled brothers and sisters are being brutalized

Spoken word is in
Keep the money and titles
I want you to comprehend
How desperate I'm feeling

Tears on my cheeks
Oppress for years and now I'm weak
Young ones looking up at me
Full of hopes and dreams

I know what I've got to do
My elders passed on the baton
The little ones
Future is in my arms so I must go on

Like Carol Lewis, I will run with this baton
Here I stand like Paul Robeson
I know my work and spoken word will touch someone
That's all that matters in the long run

WHITE MONEY (WARNING TO
PEOPLE OF COLOR ORGANIZATIONS)

Show me the money
White men on green
In debt before we're twenty
Loans for higher education
Bail too high, life in prison

Dependent on grants
Black own with white money
White foundations
Creating a new plantation
Shackles in our pockets

Tap-dancing for funders
Strings attached
The ending of the year
Hoping around like puppets
Living in an abusive relationship

Black leaders + Black issues = white money
Can't solve an equation with a problem
Master turned pimp turned corporate turned institution
He has many faces
Blending into our Black organizations

White money breaks loyalty
Leaving the community
For an office downtown
With a view of the city
Divide and concur

Uncle Sam cut welfare
And the budget
While white money flows
From Chocolate City
To the home of the Black Panthers

Trying to solve Black problems

Making revolutionaries mute
How can we keep everything Black, Malcolm.
When there are few Black philanthropists
Biting the hands that feeds?

Slave master on white money
Should remind us of our history
Unfortunately it depicts
Our present & future
Ball-n-chain in the boardroom
And in our wallets

Keeps everything the same

BROWN BROKEN BODIES

Here I stand!
but I'm not Paul Robeson
surrounded by Brown Broken Bodies
Brutality & Bullets paints Blue on Brown skin
Bruises oozing
Brothers can't run anymore
Bones snap by the swing of Batons
Four wheels equals wheelchair
Brown Broken Bodies are one thing
but Brown Broken souls are deadly
No rehabilitation
now he is weak physically and mentally
Manhood has disappeared
Heads hang down low
He is still young
but he feels & looks old

Here I stand!
holding Brown Broken Bodies on my Back
while Broken souls fills up my heart
giving me a heart attack
Wheelchairs, crutches, canes and schizophrenic minds
ex-soldiers now are ex-residents

living on the outskirts of their communities
Picking up faces from the ground
but for what?
to see more oppression
to hear racist comments
to feel systemic Blows
to stare down a Burl of a gun held by a Black & Blue
uniform
to Beg for spare charge
Mother Nature looks Better than man's society

Here I stand!
with books entitled
Why We Can't Wait & Here I Stand
but even on MLK's and Malcolm X's B-day
Brown Bodies are being abused
Going back in time so where is Harriet Tubman
cause we've dug up Masta and now he's in the White House again
Both George Washington & George Bush have a lot in common
Finishing the King Alfred Plan
James Byrd's Broken Body didn't create domestic war
But Broken Bodies in New York and Washington are being used
to send more Bodies into Battle
creating more Broken Bodies and minds

Here I stand!
shouting on an isolated island
sending out an S.O.S. to the motherland
Marcus Garvey I want to go home
Even in Africa Brothers Bodies are Broken
A disabled world nation
and I'm their spokesman
but the world won't give me a mike
so I write with my Brother's Blood
They speak to me when it is quiet at night
My book is a flood
of their wants, needs, anger and talents
Brown Broken Bodies might be scattered all over the world
but their thought patterns are unified
for a seamstress to sew together

creating a warm blanket, cradling and nursing newborns
while covering cold Brown Broken Bodies

BURIED VOICES

The next generation
Is being plucked off one by one
On the streets, in schools and in prison

Little ones snuggled
In small coffins
Buried voices have many stories

Voices from down under
Crying for their mothers and fathers
Had a lot to say but no one bothers to listen

Buried voices speaking in harmony
Tossing and turning in the grave
They want their justice

Years of abuse
Caught up in the system
And can't get loose

Black, young and disabled
Always been labeled
Home was not stable

Christopher, Seth and Dion
Blacks disabled boys can't grow up to be Black disabled men
I'm one of the chosen few

Buried in mainstream news
Buried in the community
Can't breath, can't hear, can't see

Layer after layer
Ism after ism
Wrapped up like a mummy

Buried voices rising with the morning sun
Young disabled corpse walking the earth
Talking back and heading north

Parents, teachers and politicians
Listen to the voices
They demand your attention
Buried voices
Are always with me
They are in my head guiding my pen

I write with the blood of disabled youth
I'm their agent
Writing and speaking their messages

And they told me to tell you
Many are still in pain
Bullets and fists falling down on them like pouring rain

Poems can't bring them back from the dead
Do you hear that, buried voices want me to speak the raw truth
This poem wants you to think with your heart first
then your head

The truth hurts
But it also heals
We need to get real

But I feel the tension
Every time I mention the reason
Why I wrote Buried Voices

FORBIDDEN ACTS

Drooling all over your body
you melting within my disability
erasing your fear
Sitting on my lap

intertwine like a pretzel
unravel slipping onto the floor

Hours and hours
of full body massaging
relax my cerebral palsy

Foreplay
is my spinach
giving me strength to last all night

You in my wheelchair
I'm on my knees
in between your legs, slurp mm I eat

Now I'm loose
and you know what to do
bumping & grinding

Sweet mixing with saliva
moaning and screaming
I know why you're staring at me

You just had mental sex
with a Black disabled poet
let's take it a step further

Your mind has been here before
so you know what's next
performing forbidden acts

HEADS OR TAILS

Flip it
Floating in the air
Anticipation is everywhere

Huddled over
"What is it, what is it?
It's heads!"

Tossed in the air
I hit the ground
But nobody is around

Is this a game?
Is there a referee?
Its life in America?

One side or the other side
Black or disabled
Disabled or Black

Can't be both
Take the oath
And you're American first

Hot in this melting pot
Boiling away our culture
Our brains are mashed potatoes

Identities wrapped in
Red, white and blue boxes
Traded in at the Salvation Army

I +I = I
Can't have two
You must chose only one

In court cause I've been raped
But the jury can't look at me
The judge, jury and my lawyer are all guilty

Two identities, two personalities
Flipping back and forth back and forth
No wonder I'm schizophrenic

Halloween is every day
I'm the masked man
Can't reveal the real me

Walking to the Million Man March
Wearing my Black skin but
Hiding my disability

Sitting on a picket fence
Always the last one to be chosen
Black and disabled my coin has no value

Black or disabled
My Black brothers and sisters see only one identity
Racism running rapid in the disabled community

Black History Month
Black Entertainment T.V.
Black Caucus

Black gays & lesbians
Black feminists
Black, black black black black black...

James Byrd, Black AND disabled
Margaret L. Mitchell, Black AND disabled
Marcus Hug, Black AND disabled

My people are 20 feet under and can't come back
Black Studies don't teach my history
White disabled scholars trying to write my story

Heads or tails
Hey, get real
I'm Black AND disabled

So put away that coin
I'm flipping your mind
With my dual identities

HYPNOTIZED

Follow the dollar sign
Your eyes are getting heavy
Your soul and mind is all mine

Repeat after me
"Everything is alright!"
Everything is alright
"I'll give up the fight!"
I'll give up the fight
"Be quiet and follow you to the White light!"
Be quiet and follow you to the White light

Yeah, you're almost there
Leave your anger right here
Reach, reach, step on any and everyone
Just get there
The American Dream

Climb that ladder
Higher and higher
Out of your culture
Out of your community
Out of yourself
Climbing and blending

Wake up nigger
You're hypnotized
Oh shit, am I too late?

Another Uncle Tom
Another James Connelly
Another generation gone

The media
The academic arena
The workplace
Hypnotizing you 24/7

Wake up, Motherfucker!
Your eyes are dollar signs
Uh, What! What!

Everything is all right! Right?
I mean the economy is booming
And my Brothers & Sisters are working
Right! Right! Right!
You've been hypnotized

James Byrd
Prop 209
Gentrification

But you voted for Jerry Brown
But you voted for prop 209
But you have a live-in loft
But you have stepped on James Byrd, the poor and the youth

You are in a trance
Another nigger dressed in Black skin
You are hypnotized

I got you right where I want you
Come with me
Take this money
And speak to your people
ha, ha, ha
My job is done
Time to hypnotize another one

No! No! No!
Wake up!

I KNOW, I KNOW

Lay your head on my shoulder
My sister, my sister
I know, I know

Stressed out
Fed up & beat down
Sister let it out

I know, I know
Living two lives
Very hard to survive

Sexism, racism, classism on and on
24 hours a day and seven days a week
The future looks bleak

Need to talk
Need to escape
Yeah, I know, I know

Oppress and depress
Sister can't rest
Everyday forced to be the best

Sister, talk to me
Can it be
We know what each other need

You, a woman of color
Me, a disabled man of color
But we were trained to fear, compete and not talk to each other

Share so much in common
I know, I know
Don't want to recognize our strange karma

Hard to live a lie
Too strong to cry
Why are you waving good-bye?

Stay here
Let's share our pain and fears
You got my ear

SWIMMING AGAINST THE STREAM

MMM my sperm
Here it comes
Watch out

My sperm has history swimming against the stream
My sperm has been rejected, feared, studied and labeled
     dangerous by the mainstream
My sperm has caused scientists to write books,
     Politicians to write laws and
      Doctors to write prescriptions
My sperm put the fear in Charles Darwin, slave masters and Hitler
My sperm has women running to the doctors

My sperm has been swimming against the stream

My sperm gave birth to the eugenics movement
My sperm is in test tubes marked "DAMAGED"
My sperm has been swimming in deep shark invested water
My sperm, you think could cause one, two or worst a whole
     generation like me

Oh, watch out
Here it com.....
My sperm swimming
Doing the backstroke
Mmm yeah
How can something feel so good
Be prohibited

My sperm swimming against the mainstream
My sperm is the stream
Diving in
Floating on
Riding the waves

PAINTBRUSH & A PEN WEAPONS OF TRUTH—
FRIDA & JUNE

Frida Kahlo & June Jordan
together teaching through
realism art & Poetry
Paints, paintbrushes, pens and paper
weapons of the truth
Both telling stories of the people
and their pain

Frida Kahlo in the garden with her students
June Jordan tearing down Ivory Walls with Poetry for the People
Both had a unique style of teaching
that was rooted in community
One stroke of the paintbrush opened a wound
for dark and bright colors so we can see & feel, heal & learn

Influence by their fathers
He was determine to see his daughters' strive
Father & mother planted a seed in their youthful garden
both grew up poor New York & Mexico
Kept their individuality
that attracted many
and confused their enemies

Art n Activism
Frida joined the Communist Party
June, a Black Radical
She wrote, "poetry is a political action!"
Took their art and views to their community
wrenching control from Mexico's military dictator
and college administrators
to deliver Power to the People

"You can't write lies and write good poetry!"
Yeah, she wrote the raw truth as June puts it
"because poetry is the medium for
Telling the Truth!"

June said, "to speak the truth cause
we have work to do!"
Frida painted her pain
determined to face the truth squarely
with courage & honesty

Creating an open avenue of learning
building what June calls "A Community of Trust"
This trust opened black hidden shame
that has been scratching to get out
to be replaced with pride & inner fame

A report card full of A's
A in Art, blasting revolutionary words into the market
A in Activism, blowing up the system from in and outside
A in Academia, rolling dead white history
with Poetry for the People, a rainbow at UC Berkeley

Now they are masterminding
Creating a haven for activists/artists
A resting place, palace of vibrant colors on imaginary walls
Razor sharp words producing shock and a calm atmosphere
I can't wait to get there

June & Frida taught the young
to wear their art & heart on their sleeves
A new generation armed with pens, pencils,
paintbrushes, paints & paper
Spoken, written and painted
Following their teachers, June & Frida
on their own paths to the truth

    -- Dedicated to June Jordan & Frida Kahlo

I'M SICK OF YOU!

I am sick of you!
Everywhere I go you are there
Your face is plastered in newspapers
in Hollywood, on T.V. and in bookstores

I am sick of you and your so-called movement
White disabled people everywhere
In Washington, on the big screen and academia
From the leaders to Christopher Reeves

I am sick of reading your stories
I am sick of watching your movies,
'At First Sight' and the 'Other Sister'
I am sick of your press that pumps out
WE Magazine and DSQ
I am sick of your organizations that are racist to the bone.

You is all I see, hear, and read
All about you, White disabled people
You've a monopoly on the whole industry
But that is not enough for you, now you want the minority
community.

You are slick
You told us that you'll deal with us later,
don't rock the boat and go along with the program
Now we have uncle toms that are White
because they have to be.

I'm sick of you and your phony outreach tactics
Yes, I'm sick of White disabled people in my face.
Where are my Latino, Asian, Japanese, Filipino, Latino
African, Native disabled brothers and sisters?!

I see you
hear you
read about you
for almost twenty-five years
No wonder I'm sick of you!

OH! LEROY HAS SNAPPED!

Goddamn, I wanna kill you
Put you out of your worthless existence
See blood on concrete

Drop a grenade in the Hall of Justice
Paint the White House pitch Black
Make you Black & Blue

Planet of cripples
Tip your wheelchair over
Step on you like a fucking ant

Dig you up
Open coffins
Disturbing your rest

Full of anger, hate & rage
Bringing war to the suburbs
Tie up your wife and torture your children

Split your head open like an egg
Pop, creaaaack, break your bones
Pluck your eyeballs out

Put a noose around your neck
Let you blow in the wind
With the Red, White & Blue

Rip your heart out
Through your throat
Put you on a boat

Lost at sea
Sinking in your blood
Bathing in your own feces

Oh, you thought you knew me
But everybody has a Dr. Jekyll & Mr. Hyde personality

Living in this two-faced country

Where the first President had a plantation
Where a KKK member can run for office
While Black Panthers are in prison

Dropping bombs and food on third world countries
Sending out two opposite messages
No wonder many are dual-diagnosed

Shining light on my dark side
Many think I'm way out of line
Fuck you, I'll say whatever is on my mind

Force treatment, promotion or blackmail
Won't change what I think, write and say
Words are only words, right

You should be glad I'm a poet, but you are scared
Cause I wear a three-piece suit, work a nine-to-five
And read the *Wall Street Journal* like you

My insides are boiling
Years of pretending
Are now spilling over

Can't hold it in any longer
"What's up with Leroy? He has snapped!"
Wrong person, I was never your Uncle Tom nigger

Nigger with Disability
Is not crazy
Matter-of-fact I'm pretty logical

You see, I want you on your knees
So you can view the heavenly skies for the last time
Where you're going
you won't smell Mother Nature or see her light
Cause throughout history, you got away with too many crimes

So let me stop talking
Put my words into action
There will be no funeral
Your skeleton frame & blood will evaporate in mid-air

Do you have anything to say?
No, no, shut the fuck up
Take it like a man but you are not even human
Seeing you on your knees, praying and pleading

Wow, I just had an orgasm
I'm gonna kill you
You hear me, I'm gonna kill your system

SWALLOW, SWALLOW

Swallow swallow
No time to chew
Faster faster
No time to digest
Information in seconds
Fast food fast computer

Swallow swallow
No time to think
Mainstream news in dot com culture
Hold up! Shot 19 times?
Time to move on
No time to digest the facts

Swallow, swallow
White history
Christopher Columbus, Kennedy, Princess Diana, Bush and
Clinton
Open wide
More and more
Don't you dare choke

Swallow, swallow
Stuff like a turkey
Are you constipated?
Swallow this
Oh wait
Nnnnnnnnnnnnnn
Yeah feel better

You know
What goes in
Must come out

Acknowledgments

We are only able to travel and read our poetry thanks to other people's grace and hospitality. Thank you to: Book Beat, Jaime Crespo, Jennifer Joseph, Intersection for the Arts, Diamond Dave Whitaker, Sarah Town, School of the Arts, Poor magazine, Peter Plate, Luis and Trini Rodriguez, Wanda Coleman, Sit and Spin, Chris Gual, Nettie Boulangerie, Megan Olesen and Lashen, Megan Multsaid, Graham Sheared, Donna Potts, Fools Cap Books, Spartacus Books, Red and Black Cafe, Mayworx Festival, Under the Volcano Festival, Laborfest, Steve Zeltzer, Eric Drooker, Dhai Tribe, Don Paul, Mary and Willie Ratcliff of the San Francisco Bayview newspaper, Michael Manning, and Lela Moore.